MEAT FOR MURDER

Persons this *Mystery* is about—

EARL FALKONER,
a big, vital man with a square face, deeply tanned, blond hair and the massive look of a Viking, designs very successful stage sets in Hollywood. He has built himself a huge palace of a place where he intends to write a play with the help of,

LAUREL BYRD,
a pretty young girl with dark gold hair and a major in English. She has a marvelous sense of humor and a technique for using words. The university has sent her to the Falkoner home as a writer, along with

JEFF PRINCE,
tall and lanky with blue eyes and dark wavy hair. Boyish and incredibly gallant, Jeff has serious ambitions and a great admiration for his friend,

WOODY CORNELL,
another young writer who has been everywhere and done everything, not simply out of wanderlust, but of a wise refusal to accept the standards of one time and place until he has seen them all.

ANDRÉ VIAUD,
a tiny man with short black hair, a startlingly solemn face and a subtle attitude of superiority, is a mathematical genius who is recuperating from a nervous breakdown in the isolated home of Earl Falkoner.

MRS. LOVELACE,
the thin, grayish woman who serves as Falkoner's cook and housekeeper, has a great deal of faith in the "Temple of Ultimate Revelation," and in the efficacy of roach powder.

RUTH DE LISLE,
one of those rare women who has a body instead of a figure, moves with a fluid grace. Her shining chestnut hair is wound around her head in a coil and serves to accent the perfect aquilinity of her nose.

RITA CALLENDER,
young, with long sleek legs and green eyes, is one of the "free" women of today—one of those allowed to spend both money and time as she chooses.

DENISE MORRISSEY,
a blonde with large blue eyes, a small, perfect nose and a generous mouth—painted on, is extremely fragile and ladylike. She also has money and a fondness for Falkoner.

LIEUTENANT TUCK,
of the homicide squad, is six feet five inches of sharp-witted detective. He has a long, sallowy tan face and brown eyes and he thinks there shouldn't be mirrors behind drugstore lunch counters because they take away his appetite.

BRIGIT ESTEES,
Lieutenant Tuck's assistant, is five feet eleven and wears size eight shoes. She thinks detecting is romantic. She ought to know better because her father was a cop, but she just never learned.

MEAT FOR MURDER

Things this *Mystery* is about—

• • • Three DOGS—one great DANE and two black and white spotted coach dogs . . . A sharp and shiny CARVING KNIFE . . . The PLOT for a movie script . . . Five CON-TRACTS, slightly arbitrary but absolutely legal . . . A PAM-PHLET passed out by a religious fanatic . . . A small phar-macist's box full of PHENOBARBITAL . . . A similar BOX full of something more dangerous . . . A bottle of BUTTERMILK . . . A box of ROACH POWDER . . . A quantity of TAPS FOR RATS—which means just what it says . . . Two dishes of raw HAMBURGER . . . A PHONOGRAPH without any NEEDLES . . . A VEGETARIAN who doesn't have any of the smaller vices like smoking or drinking, but must have some of the bigger ones.

Wouldn't You Like to Know—

• Why Earl Falkoner had two bodyguards?

• What he was afraid of?

• Why one bodyguard was caught chasing the cook with a carving knife?

• What the mathematician, André Viaud, was doing in the strictly artistic Falkoner house?

• Where Ruth De Lisle spent the hour and a half between 7 and 8:30 on Thursday?

• What Mrs. Lovelace found under the bed in the Red Room that gave her such a start?

• Why Earl Falkoner always drank buttermilk?

THE ANSWERS to those questions will amaze and intrigue you as you read this fast-paced story about an eccentric artist and his oddly assorted menage.

MEAT FOR MURDER

By LANGE LEWIS

Author of "Birthday Murder,"
"Juliet Dies Twice,"
"Murder Among Friends," etc.

Author's Dedication—
Dear Friends:
   This story is for you, with deepest appreciation.

                                       L. L.

WILDSIDE PRESS

MEAT FOR MURDER

List of *Exciting* Chapters—

Meat for Murder

CHAPTER ONE

THE DOGS AND THEIR MASTER

LAUREL saw at once that the drawbridge was not really a drawbridge, because it could not be raised or lowered. It spanned a flagstone courtyard, fifteen feet below the level of the road, where two stone benches with claw feet were chill in the February twilight. It led to an oak door in the base of the tower.

If this place had been built of stone instead of white stucco, she thought, it would look much more like a castle.

She glanced at Jeff. His eyes were following the high white brick wall at the road's edge, a wall which seemed to run entirely around the small estate. She glanced again at the tower, just as the oak door opened inward.

Three dogs burst out; the air was suddenly shaken with barkings as they pelted toward them. The great Dane planted his paws heavily on Laurel's shoulders and breathed foully in her face. She stood very still, staring into his amber eyes, feeling the weight of his forelegs on her shoulders, seeing the yellow teeth against the black maw which was opened in a grimace curiously like a laugh.

"Down, Pete!" said a voice. Beyond the dog's head, a tall man in dark trousers and a white shirt was crossing the bridge toward them. "They won't hurt you," he called. "Shut up!" he said to the dogs. Their barking grew more frenzied. His big hand grasped the collar of the great Dane. With no apparent effort he pulled Pete away from Laurel and dropped him.

"Come in," he said, adding, "I'll keep the dogs outside."

"Good," said Jeff, and mopped his tall forehead. "I can't say that I like dogs, or at least, not quite so many."

The big man turned and led the way to the tower. The two black-and-white-spotted coach dogs gamboled about their legs, nudging and bumping in clumsy playfulness. The great Dane followed at a slower pace; Laurel could hear his nails clicking against the timbers of the bridge.

The big man pushed open the door and held back the dogs while she and Jeff scurried into the round hall. Laurel turned in time to notice the agility with which he closed the door in the dogs' faces.

"Are you the writers from the University?" he asked.

They nodded.

"Mr. Falkoner will be a little late," he went on, as he stepped to a doorway a few feet beyond the one by which they had entered. "Please wait in here."

Laurel moved obediently toward him, and noticed that the stairway opposite the door led only down, into darkness. As she passed the tall man in the white shirt, she realized that he was *very* tall. She looked up into his face. It was an utterly impassive face, dark-browed, with light eyes. The eyes looked down at her without interest.

And then the room blazed at her, lighted by white lamps. She stepped onto the thick turquoise rug and it was like stepping onto a stage set. The vermilion leather chairs and the contrasting white chairs were grouped stiffly, the end tables which held the lamps were almost entirely made of glass, and most of the western wall of the room was a huge view window, framed by white curtains which seemed to stand like pillars rather than to hang. Between them was the twilight, empty and cold, with a few lights twinkling far below.

The only pictures were framed water-color sketches of stage sets, about which tiny painted figures postured. These were echoed in the room itself by the glass figurines on the end tables, glittering and brittle in the intense light pouring down upon them. Laurel saw nothing in the room which could not have been made day before yesterday.

She caught a fragment of a sentence. The big man was saying to Jeff, "I have to walk the dogs. They haven't had much exercise today. He likes them to have plenty of exercise. He'll be here pretty soon."

"Mind if I play some music?" asked Jeff, his eyes on the carved chest below the arm of a white chair. Laurel saw that it was not simply a chest, but a radio-phonograph as well. And on each side of the Tudor fireplace were solid shelves of record albums.

"I don't think there's any needles," the big man said. He bent over the chest to raise the lid of a tiny round box beside the turntable. "Nope. No needles. There aren't ever any needles."

"Oh," said Jeff. "Never any needles." His eyes went to those shelves of records.

"Andy has some, though," the big man said. He smiled. It was a slow smile, which hadn't even a nodding acquaintance with deep-set light eyes. "He's always playing music to himself." Wearily amused, he turned deliberately and walked out of the room into the dim round entrance hall. He turned. "I'm Jim," he said. He vanished, to reappear at once. One hand was dark against the white wall as he stared in at them around the edge of the doorway. His eyes were fixed on Jeff. "I don't like them either," he said, and once more disappeared. They heard the door boom, shut after him. It was not until she heard the clamor of the dogs that Laurel grasped what he meant.

"The dogs," she said. "He doesn't like the dogs."

"Listen!" Jeff commanded. Quite clearly they heard his voice calling, "Here, Pete! Come on now!"

They stood quite still. The barkings became fainter, carrying to their minds a picture not without sentimental overtones. A man and his dogs, going down a lonely road at dusk. But the picture was all wrong.

Then they heard the woman scream. It was a shrill scream, and it came from somewhere within the house.

Jeff's face wore an odd look, a blend of amazement and disbelief. "Shall we go and see what's wrong?" he asked.

The scream came again.

"We might as well," said Laurel equably. But her heart began to drum.

Once more in the round entrance hall, they heard for the first time sounds to indicate that they were not alone in the house. A fumble of footsteps was coming down the narrow corridor opposite the living-room. They saw a slit of light at the bottom of a door at the corridor's far end. As they approached it, the footsteps grew louder, and just as Laurel reached out to turn the knob, she heard someone breathing hard.

Then the door was open and a blaze of brightness made her squeeze her eyes shut for an instant. When she opened them, she was looking at a kitchen, a perfectly ordinary blue-and-white kitchen. Two people were standing one at each end of the white enamel table in the center of the room. The thin woman with her back to them was tensed as though wondering which way to spring; facing them was a burly young man in a sweat shirt, his tan hair bleached by the sun. He was a glowingly healthy young man, and in one hand he was holding a carving knife.

He must have seen them, but he gave no sign. Instead, he moved a stealthy inch nearer the woman in gray. She skittered a quick step in the opposite direction. Then she seemed to sense their dumfounded presence, for she turned, saw them, made an inarticulate sound and went past them like a comet with apron strings. Her gaunt face was gray; her eyes looked glazed. In the little silence that fell, door chimes sounded sweetly.

"Who are *you?*" asked the big man with the knife.

"There's a question that interests me more," Jeff said. "Why the knife?"

The big man's sun-singed eyebrows went innocently up. Then he grinned. It was a catlike grin, and eradicated his small green eyes.

"Why not?" he asked. Still grinning, he tossed the knife to the table, against which it clattered resoundingly. Laurel felt herself wince from the soles of her feet to the top of her head. The big man seemed to enjoy the wince.

"You were chasing that woman with it," said Laurel.

"Yeah. Yeah, I was chasing her. She's the cook here."

"Why were you chasing her?" asked Laurel.

The smile left the shining face. It turned sullen. "She fed my hamburger to the dogs."

"Oh," said Jeff.

The big man turned his back to them and opened the refrigerator which stood just beyond the table. Laurel caught a glimpse of a great many bottles of milk and a bunch of carrots. Jeff picked up the knife.

"Cheese!" said the man at the icebox. He turned and faced them. "You're those writers from the college."

"That's right," said Jeff.

"You shouldn't be in here." The big man's voice was accusing.

"Who are *you?*" asked Laurel.

He pointed at his unbelievably broad chest with a short tanned forefinger. "Me? I'm Tom."

"What do you do besides chase the cook?" asked Laurel.

"I'm Mr. Falkoner's bodyguard." A wary look glittered in his eye. "You shouldn't be in here. You should be in the living-room."

"I agree," said Jeff. He brought the knife with him.

Laurel looked back over her shoulder and saw only Tom's broad posterior. He was bending to examine the lower shelf of the refrigerator.

A young man in tan tweeds stood up as Laurel entered the living-room, blinked when he saw the knife in Jeff's hand. He was short and square with high shoulders and an inquiring tilt to his round brown head. Laurel found herself looking twice at his eyes. They were clear brown eyes, with heavy lids that would be good for screening private thoughts. Jeff put the knife down on a glass end table, and the young man watched him do so with a meticulous scrutiny, cocking his head just a trifle more to one side.

"What's the knife for?" he asked.

Jeff told him what they had just seen in the kitchen. The young man listened carefully. He made no comment, and Laurel felt that Jeff's story had been absorbed quite easily into a mind which accommodated such happenings without any trouble at all.

"I'm waiting for Earl Falkoner," he said. "He's late."

"We're waiting for him too," said Laurel.

"Mr. Falkoner buttonholed me at a party last night. He confronted me with the fact that I'd written a travel book. He asked me to work on a play he's writing. I agreed. I always agree. My name's Woody Cornell."

"How did you get in?" asked Laurel.

"I rang the bell. A thin woman opened the door. Then she fell down the stairs. So I came in here. I don't like it in here at all. I find myself thinking of curtains going up and down. I find myself waiting for a horde of clever people to stroll in drinking cocktails and shouting epigrams at one another."

"That's just what I felt!" said Laurel.

"This, by the way, is Laurel Byrd," said Jeff. "I'm Jeff Prince."

"Is your hair really that color?" Woody asked Laurel.

She found that one hand had gone self-consciously to the dark gold hair showing at one side of her very new hat. "Why, yes."

"You said you'd written a travel book," Jeff said. "Does that mean you're an explorer?"

"People usually say, 'Don't tell me *you're* an explorer.' Where did Falkoner buttonhole you?"

"He didn't," Jeff explained. "We've never seen him. He telephoned the head of the English Department and asked for a couple of young people who were good at dialogue. And there we were, a couple of February graduates with majors in English. What's this Falkoner like?"

"I can't remember his face," said Woody. His voice sounded puzzled, and subtly ill at ease.

"I beg your pardon," said a quiet French voice.

A tiny man was standing in the archway. Small as he was, his brown checked coat was too short in the sleeves. His short black hair had been cut by an inept barber—it was all lengths. Laurel at once classified his face as pure Celtic, a probably inaccurate label, one which called up thoughts of a pure and sensitive race going a long way back in time and untainted by any sensible blond blood. Under the three pairs of eyes, he turned on a wide, nervous smile which showed white teeth, parted in the middle. The smile went away almost at once, leaving his face startingly solemn. Laurel was vaguely troubled because she could not decide whether the perfunctory smile was habitual, or was a deliberate gesture of subtle scorn.

It was the little man in the doorway who explained his presence, rather than they theirs. "I came down for the sunken cathedral," he said.

Laurel found her eyes roving the room a little wildly. His glance toward the shelves of records put an end to her brief confusion.

"There aren't any needles," said Jeff.

"Not down here," said the little man. "But up in my room I have some. I play the music up there always. This room is not good for listening to music." He looked about him. "I think the colors take your mind out of your ears," he added thoughtfully. And then, as though conscious of having said too much, he dropped one hand into the pocket of his absurdly small coat, hunched up that shoulder in a compulsory jerk, and then went with quick neat steps to the shelves of records.

"But the staircase I saw leads only *down!*" Woody Cornell remarked emptily.

The little man continued to scan the shelves of records. "I live up in the tower," he said. "There are some stairs just across from the kitchen door. I imagine the tower was intended to be one of the servants' rooms."

Woody Cornell went to the little man standing small and a trifle shabby with the bindings of the albums bright beyond his black and rumpled head. He put out his hand. "My name's Cornell."

They shook hands briefly, and Laurel saw that the small man's hand was like a child's. "My name is André Viaud," he said, and the way in which his tongue gave the name the sound it had in his own country was sad and nice and quite unconsciously so.

"We're waiting for your friend Falkoner," Woody explained.

Laurel was sure she saw a scarcely perceptible tightening of André Viaud's mouth, as though to hold back certain words which second thought had told him had better not be spoken. "You're the writers," he said, instead. "You're going to work on his play with him. That will be an experience."

"He hasn't hired us yet," Jeff said, as he lighted a cigarette and looked about for a place to put the match.

"He will." André Viaud's eyes were obscurely amused.

Before Laurel had time to search her mind for a possible reason for that inward laughter, they heard the powerful roar of a car stopping in front of the house. The sound was choked off almost at once; the silence was followed by the powerful chunk of a car door closing. André Viaud quickly turned and took a purple album from the second shelf; he carried it to the archway under one arm as a schoolboy carries his books. He turned in the archway long enough to say, "I am very happy to have met you," and then his narrow checked shoulders crossed the dim round entrance hall to the corridor leading back toward the kitchen. They heard the muffled patter of feet ascending the flight of stairs.

At the same time someone crossed the bridge outside with a heavy, rapid, solid tread. There was a faint creak as the front door was opened, and then the heavy tread was in the round entrance hall. The wide arch which had just framed André Vaud's retreating figure now held a new figure, in an excellently tailored gray flannel suit, coming toward them.

The man's square face was deeply tanned. The lower lip was square too, and against the deep color of the face it looked bloodless. He was not massive enough to make Laurel think immediately of a Viking, but his blond hair and eyebrows, and his predatory cold eyes, and especially the vitality of the sure, heavy tread forced Laurel's brain to frame the word Viking as a second thought. And then her mind said, *No! No! Anglo-Saxon. The helmet with the two curved horns.*

He reached Woody and put out a hand. It was very tan below the gray sleeve and the narrow strip of white cuff. "How are you, Mr. Cornell?" he said. His voice was brusque and businesslike, and flat and strained, and his perfunctory smile showed square teeth which had been preserved by an expensive dentist. Laurel noticed that his hair was gray at the temples. And then those chill eyes were on hers. The look he gave her was disturbing because it seemed to classify her on the basis of externals only. She found her hand in his. "Miss Byrd," he said. For a moment their eyes locked as their hands had, and she absurdly wanted to say, *You're wrong! I'm not a nice little thing in a green suit!* But his hand was gone as suddenly as it had clasped hers, and he was looking at Jeff, who was taking an extremely nonchalant puff of his cigarette. "Out!" he said. "Either the cigarette or you." He gave a short hard laugh, meant to be conciliatory, and added, "A very bad habit. Every habit should serve a purpose. Smoking dims your wits and rots your lungs." Firmly, he pinched Jeff's cigarette between his fingers, carried it at arm's length to the Tudor fireplace, and tossed it into the logs.

Jeff's face was a deep pink.

Woody said, "I've heard that people who have none of the small vices always have one of the big ones."

Falkoner's icy eyes went to his face. Falkoner

showed his porcelain-white front teeth. Then he jammed his hands into his pockets and strode toward the fireplace. Laurel noticed for the first time that he was wearing tan huaraches instead of shoes. They were defiantly out of place with the neat gray suit.

Falkoner stood brooding down at the logs for a moment. Then he turned and faced them. His eyes challenged each of their faces in turn, and he said, "Ideas are the most precious things in the world." He turned to the fireplace and put out the round dying ember of Jeff's cigarette with the toe of one sandal. He began to pace up and down the hearth, his eyes sometimes on the vast view window with the night pressing flat against it, and sometimes on one or the other of their faces. His strained voice seemed to hint of some inward pressure which was pushing him on from minute to minute to this place and that; some pressure that was with him even as he slept and had always been with him and always would be. A man in love with a wanton who was slowly killing him would have a voice like that. Or perhaps a man in love with success.

"My ideas are my ideas, your ideas are your ideas, Joe Doakes's ideas are his ideas, and there is nothing I can think of that's more lousy than stealing another man's ideas. The ideas I discuss tonight are my ideas and if you work with me they will merge with your ideas and out of that will come a story, a big story, a story which will make us all a lot of money. I'm a busy man and writing takes time—all art takes time—art is long and life is short—a lot shorter if you smoke cigarettes, but short enough anyway. That's why I need you. I'm an artist—an artist with color and line, I mean. But I learned this a long time ago: that the things that make a good stage set—I design stage sets—that's my job, that's what I do—will also make a good story." He paused and said carefully, "I've never sold a story for less than $10,000."

He let that sink in. His eyes fell on the carving knife which Jeff had laid on one of the small tables that held one of the white lamps which lighted the room. "What's that doing here?" he asked.

"Your bodyguard was chasing the cook with it, so I took it away with me," said Jeff smoothly, watching with disguised eagerness for Falkoner's reaction.

Falkoner went over and picked up the knife. Holding it casually in one hand he went to the archway. "Tom!" he called.

He turned back toward them. "So if I don't hire you I want you to understand that whatever we discuss tonight belongs to me and is not to be used by you in any way."

Laurel felt a sense of profound indignity in her throat. "We are above plagiarism, Mr. Falkoner, believe me," she heard herself say.

He met her eyes with his own cold ones. "Good," he said.

Tom hulked large in the doorway. Falkoner handed him the knife, point first. "Don't chase Mrs. Lovelace any more," he commanded. "And tell her we're ready to eat dinner now, and bring me the contracts."

"O. K.," said Tom, and hulked out again with the peculiar tight gait of the muscle-bound.

Falkoner turned back to them. "He has a helluva funny sense of humor," he explained, his disinterested eyes on the black pane of the window with the night pressing against it. He again went to the fireplace and stood there very solidly on his ridiculous sandals, his hands jammed again into his pockets. The quality in the man that made it hard for him to stay in one place showed itself now in his eyes, which prowled about the room and across their faces while that strained voice struggled with every sentence.

"This play of mine," he said, "is, I think, pretty different. There's this woman, you see, and she's not a type. Nothing chi-chi. Nothing—" He made a groping gesture with one of those dark square hands. "Nothing, well, chi-chi. Except maybe that she's in love. Two men. One alive, one dead."

He stopped talking and stared hard at each of them in turn. Laurel stifled a desire to say, *I believe that's been done, you know.*

Falkoner went on: "The dead man's her husband—financial wizard—money begets money—that kind of guy. The other guy is a protégé—" he gave them the word with a little touch of pride in his voice—"of her husband's. Young doctor. And no Kildare stuff. He's ten or even twelve years younger than she is, and that's a new angle, because they're the love affair. So in order to carry out her husband's dying wishes, she continues to see that the doctor gets the money for his medical training, which is hard for him to take—not the money so much as the fact that she's the one who's giving it to him, because he's in love with her in a perfectly nice way, but he doesn't know that the wizard lost most of his fortune in the market crash—did I tell you that? We might open the story with a nice montage of Black Friday, a guy jumping out of a window."

"Oh, then it's going to be a movie script," said Laurel.

Falkoner looked at her hard. "Of course," he said, irritated and amazed. He looked at Woody and then at Jeff. "Finally, after a lot of things happen, the woman gets together with the doctor. The audience will want that from the start, and finally we give it to them, after a lot of things happen. . . ."

Tom came in with a long sheaf of papers in one hand, the hand that had held the carving knife. "Mrs. Lovelace says dinner gonna be ready in ten minutes. Boy, am I hungry!"

Ignoring him, Falkoner took the sheaf of papers. Tom ambled out. Falkoner dealt each of them a contract. "Read 'em over," he said almost genially.

Laurel was a little astonished to see her name at the head of the contract, although it had been spelled *Bird.* She realized at once that he had got their names from the head of the English Department when he telephoned that morning.

"My name is spelled with a *y*," she told him.

He came to her side drawing a thick gold fountain pen from his breast pocket. He changed the *i* to *y*. "Initial it," he told her. She dutifully initialed the change, and went on reading.

Stripped of its legal verbiage, the first long paragraph of the contract seemed to say that Laurel Byrd, the party of the second part, agreed to collaborate with Earl Falkoner, the party of the first part, in the writing of a play for the sum of $250 when the play had been completed to the satisfaction of the party of the first part, plus a one-sixth interest in the play. She closed her eyes to do a bit of mental arithmetic and came to the conclusion that she and Jeff and Woody together had a half interest in the script. Falkoner, then, had the other half. She opened her eyes and saw him looking at her. "It's fair," he assured her; "I have the idea and the sale for the story." She nodded.

The second paragraph stopped her in mid-nod: *The party of the second part further agrees to reside with the party of the first part until the play shall be completed, for the great economy of time this arrangement will effect.* She hastily looked up at Falkoner, her mouth open for an objection.

Again Falkoner seemed to know what she was going to say. "All very regular," he informed her coldly. "Your room is next to Mrs. Lovelace's. Chaperon. And there's a lock on the door if you're that type."

This made her feel silly. She finished reading the contract, conscious more of the blood which had rushed to her cheeks than of the words before her eyes.

She lowered the contract to her lap just as Jeff did the same. Woody, she saw, was carefully folding his across its two original creases. "Of course," he said brightly, "there'll be plenty of time for us to discuss the terms you mention here while you're deciding to hire us."

"I've already decided to hire you," said Falkoner shortly.

Laurel found herself remembering little André Viaud's secret smile.

Falkoner turned to take a red leather box from the mantel, which he slid open with an easy movement of his brown hands. He took out a kitchen match, and squatted before the stack of logs on the grate. "Talk it over before you sign," he suggested, largely over his shoulder. He struck the match on the bottom of the box, and held it to the cluster of thin wood below the logs. In a moment a rag of orange flame fluttered up across the log's gray bark. Falkoner stood up. He went to the white door in the same wall as the window, which he opened, and stood aside. "You'll probably want to talk it over privately," he said.

Laurel walked toward him, feeling Jeff and Woody at her heels, and, at a nod from Falkoner, stepped through the door and drew her breath.

She was standing on the upper landing of a flight of outer stairs leading down the wall of the house. It led to a huge semicircular cement terrace, surrounded by a balustrade of the conventional squat stone urns and lighted by half a dozen square lanterns which rose from the wide upper surface of the surrounding wall on tall wrought-iron stems. Below the balustrade the hill sloped down into the darkness of a little valley; beyond that more hills were one shade darker than the wide western sky in which a few stars glowed cold and bright.

She turned to Falkoner and saw in his impassive face no appreciation of what had moved her so.

The three of them clicked down the cement stairs, and Falkoner turned back to the living-room, closing the white door after him.

"It makes you think of star-crossed lovers, doesn't it?" Laurel said. "The tryst by moonlight, with disaster waiting in the castle, ready to tread remorselessly down the steps."

"Exactly," Jeff said.

They walked to the cement wall, and leaned their elbows on it.

"What's wrong here?" asked Woody abruptly.

"What do you mean?" asked Jeff.

"I don't know," said Woody, his face forlorn in the light of the lanterns.

"What do you two think of the contract?" asked Laurel.

"Seems fair enough," said Woody carefully.

"I don't like that business about living here," said Laurel.

"Oh, *that!*" said Woody. "That doesn't bother me. We'd lose too much time winding our way up from Hollywood. What I don't like is that clause 'finished to the satisfaction of the party of the first part.'"

"But look!" urged Jeff. "It's to his advantage as well as ours to get the thing ready for sale as soon as possible. That doesn't bother me at all. What bothers me is this. Apparently this bird Falkoner is violently against smoking. I've smoked ever since I was fifteen and I like to smoke, and I can't work without a cigarette in the tray beside my typewriter, and I'm not going to learn any new tricks at my age. He has fat thumbs."

"He doesn't have fat thumbs," said Laurel, laughing, "just square."

"He should have fat thumbs," said Jeff darkly.

"Why not toss a coin?" suggested Woody. "We each have a reason—maybe because we're all hungry—for not quite liking the idea of working for Mr. Falkoner. On the other hand, we have nothing else to do just now. And frankly, I could use my share of the money toward my trip to Martinique—I'm going to look into voodoo." He took a half dollar from his pocket and held it out, flat and silver on his palm.

Laurel picked it up. "Heads voo doo, tails we don't," she said.

Woody and Jeff looked at each other and grinned and groaned, and Laurel spun the coin into the air and caught it with a flat, spanking sound on her palm. Their three heads bent over it.

"Voo doo," said Woody.

They wheeled together and started back toward the stairs. They saw the three cots under the slope of the staircase at the same moment. They were snugly made with brown Army blankets, and stood in a neat row.

Jeff's voice was full of foolishness. "Someone's been sleeping in my bed, Goldilocks chirped, but the son of a gun got away."

Laurel threw back her head in a laugh and saw the wide pane of the window backed now not by darkness but by light. Brilliant, fluctuating light, made by the flames in the fireplace, and square and stolid in the middle of it, Falkoner's dark shape, hands in pockets, looking down at them.

Falkoner sat at the head of the table, André at the foot; Laurel, Jeff and Woody shared one side, Tom and Jim the other. Mrs. Lovelace moved gray and silent around the board in the wavering and dignified light of the tall pale candles in the great silver candelabra. When she set down a huge platter of lamb chops, her thin hands shook.

Falkoner ate a head of lettuce which he quartered competently with the carving knife, five stalks of celery, three raw carrots and a glass containing a pint of buttermilk. His square jaws masticated hugely, his eyes roved from face to face. Pete, the great Dane, sat and watched the two big men eat lamb chops, and occasionally snuffed up an imaginary crumb from the floor.

Falkoner spoke to Jim. "You'll have to give him a bath," he said, around a mouthful of lettuce. "He's beginning to smell again." Jim nodded and went on chewing.

Suddenly Falkoner pointed at André with his fork. "Eat your dinner," he commanded.

André put down his knife. His shoulder hunched; he dropped his hand into the side pocket of his coat. He stood up. He walked the length of the table to the archway with the dim round hall beyond it. Falkoner half turned his head to watch him.

"No," said André, and went away.

The two big men turned their heads in perfect synchronization and looked at the empty doorway. They looked at Falkoner. They looked down at their plates and ate again.

Falkoner's face was dark under his tan. "Mrs. Lovelace!" he called. The door to the kitchen opened instantly. "Bring me some more buttermilk," he said. "And take away Mr. Viaud's plate."

She could not have explained how, but Laurel knew that she had seen something quietly momentous happen there in the candlelight.

JEFF arrived at nine the next morning. As he swung Laurel's two suitcases into the turtle of his car, he asked, "What did Bertine say about it all?"

As an answer she showed him the note which Professor Bertine Pratt of the Department of English, whose flat she had shared for the past six months, had left on the pillow of Laurel's bed.

Byrd, Dear: I'm celebrating the start of my sabbatical leave with a quick trip to San Francisco. I plan to buy the craziest hat in town. The visiting professor and his wife definitely want to sublet the flat. I think in about a week. Does that disrupt your plans too much? I'll write. Bertine.

"Well," said Jeff brightly. "Falkoner's offer of bed and board comes in nicely, doesn't it?"

"Beautifully," agreed Laurel bleakly.

"Works well for me, too. The fraternity house has a waiting list a block long. They cheered when I told them I was moving out."

They were both rather silent as they drove out Western Avenue toward the blue hills of Hollywood.

Woody opened the front door of the house on the hill. He led them down the stairs.

"This place is strange and wonderful," he said. "Jeff, you and I share a bedroom so nautical that I was seasick most of the night. I wish I'd stayed at the hotel. Laurel, your room's done in horror blue and ox-skull white. You'll love it. Falkoner appeared this morning in a yachting cap. He's gone to the beach. It seems that he swims three miles a day. The muscle men came to breakfast in swimming trunks, but they stayed here. And Mrs. Lovelace slipped me this with my orange juice." .

"This" was a tiny pamphlet, four inches by two inches, bearing the title *Four Things That God Wants You to Know*. Laurel opened it and leafed through and saw that someone, presumably Mrs. Lovelace, had encircled in pencil the quotation: *For what shall it profit a man, if he shall gain the whole world, and lose his own soul?—Mark* 8:36.

"So stow away your duffle," Woody said, "and we'll get down to the lady, the doctor and the market crash."

As Laurel laid the last pink slip away in the middle drawer, Woody and Jeff appeared in the doorway. Jeff was lighting a cigarette.

"You've seen nothing yet," promised Woody. "We work in the Red Room. Come on."

The Red Room was the master bedroom, directly below the living-room, but smaller because of a large bathroom and dressing-room. The walls were sand color; the furniture, which included a big square desk with a typewriter, was dark and heavy; the bed was a four-poster. The rug and the bed's satin spread, and the three deep armchairs, were red. There was a fireplace, as in the room above. A window in the right wall, beside the fireplace, looked onto the grim flagstoned courtyard below the bridge. A French door in the opposite wall opened onto the semicircular terrace where the three of them had tossed the coin the night before. Laurel had just oriented herself when a loud grunt, followed by a muffled thud, came from the sunlit terrace.

"I forgot to tell you," said Woody. "They wrestle."

Laurel went quickly to the doorway, and stopped.

On a huge mat at the center of the terrace, Jim and Tom were engaged in a titanic struggle. Muscles bulged under their bronzed skins; sweat ran down their strained faces. As she watched, Jim's long and powerful legs locked around Tom's thick waist in what she believed was known as a scissors lock, and all at once Tom turned into the professional wrestler of many jokes. His mouth opened in a big oval of anguish, his fists beat a tattoo on the mat. Jim's body strained and sweated as he exerted still more pressure.

"He's not kidding," said a quiet voice behind her, and she turned to see Woody's round face looking out at the sunlight unsmilingly, the brown eyes alert under their sleepy lids.

"All right!" Tom groaned. "O. K.! O. K.!"

Jim tightened his legs in a last triumphant and terrible pressure, and then he unlocked them and got to his feet. His face was utterly expressionless as he looked down at Tom, who was slowly shaking his head with its forelock of sun-yellowed hair. Then he looked up at Jim. "Don't tell him," he said hoarsely.

Jim continued to watch Tom, who got carefully to his feet.

"Don't tell him," Tom pleaded once more.

"Maybe I will and maybe I won't," said Jim in his civil voice. Then he turned toward where Laurel was standing. Seeing her there he stopped for a moment, and then continued toward the Red Room. As she stepped hastily away from the French door, he passed from the sunlight into the dark room, where his body seemed suddenly very naked. A healthy animal smell of sweat accompanied him. "Good morning," he said, and made for the bathroom.

"Good morning," she echoed, and heard Jeff's voice like a shadow of her own. Tom followed in a moment, his red face surly, rubbing a mark on his upper arm that looked like a burn. He said nothing but went out of the room into the lower hall, round and dim like the entrance hall on the floor above.

Jim peered at them through the half-opened bath-room door (the tiles were vermilion). "He's going to use the shower in your room, if that's O. K.," he informed Woody and Jeff. "He always has."

Woody made a lavish gesture. "The more the merrier," he said.

Jim closed the bathroom door.

At eleven o'clock Falkoner returned, wearing his huaraches, gray slacks, a tweed coat of robin's-egg blue with a maroon scarf tied loosely at the throat, and a navy-blue yachting cap.

They had just decided how to use the market-crash montage. After some discussion Woody had summed up their decision. "Then it's agreed that we'll pick up each of the central characters just as he learns the bad news. The wizard in his Wall Street office; the wife in her parlor; the doctor in his interne's outfit at the hospital, the only one it doesn't touch."

"Right," agreed Jeff and Laurel.

Falkoner lay down on the scarlet satin bedspread, crossed his ankles, clasped his hands under his head, closed his eyes. "I've thought of what to do with the market-crash montage," he announced.

"So have we," said Laurel cheerfully.

He opened his eyes, looked at her without seeing her, closed his eyes again. "The camera pans up a tall building. It stops at one window after another. A different scene inside each one. The butcher, the baker and the candlestick maker, all reacting."

"Oh," said Woody. "And among them the characters who later appear in the story!"

"No. None of them ever appears in the story again. That's what's different. That's what makes it good!"

"But it'll take ten or fifteen minutes' time for so

many scenes," Laurel protested.

"That depends on how fast you write it," said Falkoner, not opening his eyes.

Jeff looked at Laurel. Laurel looked at Woody. Woody looked at the ceiling.

Falkoner talked. His voice was still strained, his sentences still ramified madly or died at birth. He talked for two hours. The phone beside the bed rang three times. The first time it rang, Falkoner went right on talking. Laurel's nerves cringed at each of the following four rings. Then the ringing stopped and in a moment Mrs. Lovelace's thin voice echoed down the stair well. "Miss Callender calling."

Falkoner thought briefly, then reached out and took the phone from its cradle. "Yes," he said, brusquely. "No. . . . No. . . . No, Rita. . . . All right." He replaced the phone and picked up the rest of his sentence.

In half an hour the phone rang a second time. "Mr. Larry Harvers," called Mrs. Lovelace's voice down the stair well. "I'm not at home," Falkoner called back. The third time the phone rang, Mrs. Lovelace called, "Ruth De Lisle."

Falkoner snatched the phone. "Hello, Ruth. . . . Fine. Yes. . . . Yes. . . . Yes. Absolutely. . . . No, Denise isn't back. Not for a month or so, I'm sure. . . . Oh, she did?" He gave his iron laugh. "Swell. . . . All right. Good-by."

"Did Mrs. Lovelace say that was Ruth De Lisle?" asked Woody.

Falkoner nodded.

"I'll have to give her a ring," murmured Woody vaguely. "I thought she was in Bermuda."

"You know her?" asked Falkoner, his blond brows surprised.

"She and my mother attended an old French convent together in their girlhood," Woody said gravely.

Falkoner darted him a look of fierce suspicion, and turned to Laurel. "Where was I?"

She looked down at her notes. "You were at a bridge party, in the home of Emily Ives, on the day the market crashed," she told him.

"Well, let's have lunch," said Falkoner.

Lunch was a large vegetable salad, celery, raw carrots, 100% whole wheat bread, and a pint of milk apiece. André was not there. They could hear the *Valse Triste* weeping in his room above the round hall.

"André's a mathematical genius," announced Falkoner abruptly. "Just getting over a nervous breakdown. I suggested that he stay here while he recuperated and get some healthy living for a change." His eyes went to Jeff. "He's one of the cigarette-and-coffee boys too," he said.

Laurel found herself wondering whether living in the house on the hill was quite the best treatment for a nervous breakdown.

Falkoner talked for two hours more, and then went away. They wrestled the first scene into order, briefed the plot of the entire story, briefed the backgrounds of the three chief characters, and it was time for dinner, which was like dinner the night before, except that Woody told a story about his last trip to Indo-China, and André told how the first English words he had learned, at fourteen, were "Hello, Yonkee!" So now, thought Laurel, he must be thirty-four or -five. He looks twenty.

The large glass of milk which was served her with dinner made Laurel very sleepy. She could feel her lids drooping when she rose from the table. But she went resolutely down to the Red Room with Jeff and Woody to continue work on the play.

They made a fire, and with the flames hot on her shins she sat in front of it, and dreamily heard Woody say, "What the story needs is a good healthy villain. Everyone is much too nice."

She jumped to her feet, with a tremendous effort. "I need coffee," she said. "Strong, black coffee."

Jeff stood up too. "So do I," he announced. "My mouth is full of a lactic taste."

"We'll go up to the kitchen and persuade Mrs. Lovelace," Woody decided.

But in the lower round hall they realized that they were on their own, because light was coming from under the door of Mrs. Lovelace's room at the far end of the lower corridor. A mournful choir was singing, "Are you washed in the blood of the Lamb?"

"Does she hold revival meetings, or has she a radio?" wondered Woody.

"She can have a sixty-piece band under the bed," said Jeff, "so long as she has coffee in the kitchen cupboard."

There was coffee in the cupboard. A two-pound tin.

"Probably decaffeinated," Jeff said.

"Let's hurry," suggested Laurel, looking over her shoulder.

Jeff made the coffee. They drank it with surreptitious glee. "I feel as though I were smoking opium," confessed Laurel, looking over her shoulder for the fourth time.

"I don't think he would really care," said Woody, and they all knew of whom he spoke. "If he walked through that door and caught us with the signs of our revelry upon us, he wouldn't really care. He's messianic only in a small way; he doesn't have time to do the thing on a large scale. He feeds the muscle men and the dogs and us with meat because he doesn't care enough about any of us to try to woo us to his better way of life. He doesn't give a hoot about reforming the world; he only wants to grab it by the tail for himself, and he thinks vegetables will help him grab."

"But he objected to my smoking," Jeff said.

"That was to show who was boss," Woody replied.

It made Laurel a little nervous, this verbal dissection of their host and their employer in his own kitchen. "We still need a villain," she said, to change the subject.

"Why isn't there a villain? That's what bothers me so," Woody said.

"What do you mean?" asked Laurel bluntly. The kitchen was cold; she felt the skin of her forearms prickle into goose flesh.

"It tells me so much about him," Woody said, with his eyes half shut, and in a faraway voice. "First, that he has never heard about the old law that there is no drama without conflict; but second, and more important, that he may be one of those people who don't know what evil is."

Laurel experienced a sense of unreality standing there in that ordinary blue-and-white kitchen with the copper pots above the stove. The contrast between the setting and those quiet words of Woody's was dreamlike in its calm ridiculousness.

"Let's go down to the Red Room and talk about werewolves," she suggested dryly.

Woody opened his eyes. "I met a werewolf face to face in Paris one night," he said earnestly. "Did I ever tell you about it?"

Laurel laughed.

"I mean it," said Woody. "He had long fangs with blood on them and he came toward me in the lamplight on all fours. He was wearing an opera cape."

"What did you do?" asked Jeff, half-smiling, half-curious.

"I ran," said Woody. "But I took a good look first. That's why I was able to identify him at the police station the next day. They booked him for having killed a little girl by biting through her jugular vein. Her body was lying in the alley that night."

"Oh, he was crazy!" said Laurel, relieved to find herself on solid ground again. "He thought he was a werewolf!"

"Does that explain very much?" asked Woody gently.

In the Red Room they discussed the problem of making believable the fact that Emily Ives was in love with two men, one of them dead.

In the little pause that fell while Laurel was trying to decide just how long Walter and Emily Ives had been married, and whether it would be better to bless the union with a child, Jeff announced, "Emily Ives gives me the hives."

Woody said, "What in the name of heaven is that?"

Laurel saw that he was staring at the French windows that led onto the semicircular terrace. A terrible face was glaring in at them through the middle pane.

"It's only Pete," she realized, synonomously with a thrill of fear.

"What do you mean, 'only'?" Jeff said, and went over to make sure the window was securely latched.

"The blond man in the big house, with the big bodyguard and the big right-hand man and the big dog and the frightened cook, and the little man in the tower—I don't like it," said Woody from the depths of one of the red chairs.

The door leading to the lower hall opened and André Viaud came in quietly. He was wearing a maroon flannel bathrobe and looked a little startled at seeing them.

"Oh," he said. He started to back out. "I came down to clean my teeth."

Laurel stood up. "We're stale on the story. I'm going to turn in. I won't sleep. I shouldn't have had that third cup of coffee."

Rather like a magician, André was suddenly holding out a tan pharmacist's box opened on his palm. He turned his smile on and off uncertainly. "Phenobarbital," he said.

The word made no sense in Laurel's weary, keyed-up brain.

André took three steps toward her, still offering her the box. For the first time she was aware of the force behind his clear hazel eyes. Suddenly they chimed with the intelligent wide brow; she realized that she was looking at a man who was a person in his own right, a man who could not be classified as human scenery in a very curious house. With his eyes on hers, she was suddenly aware that she rather liked André. Perhaps the fact that he was offering something to her, was making a timeless gesture of friendship, the tangible gesture of giving, was tricking her. But for that moment she thought that he also liked her. She had the notion that during the two dinners they had eaten at the same table, he had watched her when she had not known it, and had liked what he had seen.

"Phenobarbital," he repeated. "One of the milder narcotics. My doctor prescribed these for me. I do not sleep very well. You swallow one with a glass of water half an hour before you go to bed."

She looked from his face to the box. She saw a dozen or so clear small capsules containing a white powder. "Thank you, André," she said, and took one.

He closed the box and put it into the pocket of his bathrobe. "You may find yourself needing one again," he said. "Please let me know if you do." With a certain dignity, he turned then and went toward the bathroom with the vermilion tiles, the cord of his robe trailing after him.

She took the capsule in the bathroom between her room and Mrs. Lovelace's, and then went about her nightly ritual of cold cream, bobby pins, toothpaste, with an awareness of being in a strange room in a strange house, a long way from home. She turned out the bed lamp and had just given a first shiver at the touch of the cold clean sheets when she realized that she had not opened the window. It was a casement window, and as she pushed it out, she chanced to look down.

Her room was below the dining-room, and the window looked out across the terrace, the view somewhat impeded by the underside of the flight of stairs leading down from the living-room.

Below the staircase, she saw again the three cots. In the cots, their sleeping faces blank in the starlight, were Jim, Falkoner and Tom.

Lying in the darkness, she felt wide-awake. *That stuff won't work*, she told herself. *I should have taken two*. Then she smiled and thought of the doctor who had once said to her, "I dislike prescribing drugs to women. They all seem to go on the theory that if one pill will do them good, two will do twice as much good. And that's never true."

She was thinking quite lucidly of this one moment, and then she was looking at the sunlight outside the window.

BERTINE, DEAR: *Thanks for your letter. I'm glad that you've decided to spend another week in S. F.; after several years of Freshman English, faculty meetings and the Victorian Period, you deserve a whirl. Before I left that flat I put the things I would not be needing in the hall closet along with yours, so the suggestion in your letter was acted upon before I received it. I'm sure also that Professor Smollett and his wife won't need that closet.*

I am living in Hollywood at the home of a man named Falkoner. It's not as wicked as it sounds—I'm working on a play for him. Jeff is here too, and an explorer named Woody Cornell whom I already adore. He's the only son of one of these wealthy and conservative old California families—the homestead is near San Francisco. His great-great-grandfather knew what the inside of a covered wagon looked like; a greater grandfather than that left the Cavaliers and Roundheads to fight things out the best they could and had built a house in Virginia by the time Charles II reached the throne of England. I think that the need for new horizons is a primal need with Woody, born not of incompleteness within himself, as is so often the case with these wanderlust boys, but rather of a wise refusal to accept the standards of one time and place until he has seen them all. He has wizard's eyes and he smiles like a cherub and I have the feeling about him that whatever stars he may fall asleep beneath, he will wake up full of hunger for strange ones. I seem to be waxing lyric, which will give you the false impression that I'm in love with him, so I shall hasten to add that he's all of five feet six, has little or no neck and a slight lisp, and believes quite matter-of-factly in werewolves, vampires and all the things that go boomp in the night.

Jeff you know—imagine him working for a vegetarian who does not approve of coffee, alcohol or smoking!

I can't quite make Falkoner out. For all his rugged ways, there's something about him which vaguely suggests decadence. The room where we do our work is the master bedroom of the house, and his room, although he sleeps outdoors. And there is a wealthy masculine odor of unguents and after-shave lotions to the place that makes me think of late Rome. Also, he has in one corner a pigskin-covered, chromium-legged massage table on which his blond henchman kneads him occasionally. Also, he has The Thing. At first glance, Jeff and Woody and I took it to be a lamp of some sort. But it isn't. Falkoner called us in last night for a conference about the play. He was sitting beneath The Thing; the large chromium bowl was fitted to his head by means of a heavy rubber edging that went around it like a beret. He began to talk, and clicked a switch. With a low, wheezing sound, something like the noise of a vacuum cleaner, the cup rose from his head, sucking his face up with it (the rubber edging clinging firmly) into a look of wild amazement. After several seconds, and with another wheeze, the chromium bowl plopped abruptly down onto his head, pushing his face together into a deep scowl. This went on and on, and with genuine unconcern Falkoner went on and on too, shouting above the noise.

That little scene gives you a better idea of the man and his house than almost anything else I could tell you. I should, perhaps, mention that there are two muscle men here, who do odd jobs and wrestle with each other in between times. The dark one never makes a sound when

*he walks. Woody pretends to be rather alarmed by him.
He said today at breakfast, "I will be in the bathroom,
I will have the toothpaste on my brush, I will start to
brush my teeth, I will glance at the mirror above the
basin, and there is Jim behind me, with his arms folded
over his chest."*

*The blond muscle man just grins. It is a Cheshire Cat
sort of grin.*

*Perhaps I should mention the dogs. There are three
dogs here, two black-and-white spotted coach dogs, the
sort of dogs who have stupid bumps on their craniums,
and a great Dane. They are constantly hungry. If so
much as a crumb of anything that looks edible falls to the
floor they are right there jostling one another. The great
Dane usually wins. He licks his chops with a flapping
sound, and looks sad.*

*And the cook could step from the wings of any theater
and play the Third Witch without benefit of make-up;
and a little mathematician lives in the tower, waiting, no
doubt, for the Marines to arrive.*

*Well, darling, this is an epistle. But we're at the end
of our rope as far as the play is concerned. When Falkoner comes back from his three-mile swim we will read
him what we have written, he will say, "Swell, swell, swell,
but I got a new idea just as I passed the pier," and we'll
rewrite everything.*

*Jeff and Woody, when I last saw them, were lying on
their backs in the garden. The grass slopes so abruptly
that they looked as though they might slide gently down
to the lower wall at any moment. Jeff was smelling a yellow rose, and they looked very much like two young men
talking about Life. I believe I shall join them. Laurel.*

But she didn't. As she pulled the last sheet of her
letter from the typewriter, she heard music pouring down
the stairs from the living-room. "God bless André for
those phonograph needles," she said to the blue walls of

her room, and went upstairs.

A young woman was slumped deep in one of the white chairs. She was wearing white linen tennis shorts and a persimmon-red shirt and was looking pensively at her legs, stretched out sleek and tan and bare from the white chair. Her red-nailed hands were clasped across her stomach. She sat there, very much at home, listening to *Rhapsody in Blue*. As Laurel entered the room, she looked up, and said in a low and pleasantly husky voice, "Who the hell are you?"

There was only one possible answer. "Who the hell are *you?*" Laurel replied.

"My name is Callender," said the woman in the chair.

"My name is Byrd," said Laurel.

Callender looked up again, and Laurel was dumfounded to see tears glittering in her eyes. "Turn that thing off, will you?" she pleaded, her voice so low that Laurel barely heard her. "It's killing me!" She fished blindly into a big white purse beside her in the chair and then wiped carefully around her mascara with a piece of pink Kleenex.

Laurel went obediently to the big chest, lifted the needle from the black disk, and snapped the switch which turned off the machine. Then she sat down on the red chair beside it, facing the white chair where Callender was sitting, and waited for enlightenment. In the silence that followed the cessation of the music, she became gradually aware of the smell of whisky.

"I heard you coming up the stairs," Callender said. "You live here." It was not a question. It was a statement.

"Yes."

"Relation?" The question was doubtful.

"No."

"No. Mrs. Lovelace let me in and she told me he wasn't, but I thought I might as well make sure. Do you expect him back soon?"

"I never expect him until he appears."

"Yes. I know." Callender looked at her knees and Laurel looked at her. The girl's white eyelids now concealed eyes which were no real color at all. They weren't an honest brown, but they had some brown in them. They had also a greenish look. Laurel remembered where she had seen that peculiar shade before. It was in a shadowed stretch of shallow stream. Callender's face had none of the healthy quality of the long and beautiful legs. She was smoothly powdered over a foundation cream and, in contrast to the rest of her, the face was much too pale. A dull paleness. She had a vermilion mouth that might be any kind of mouth at all. At present it looked merely sullen. Her nose was very small, almost a pug, but her forehead was broad and intelligent, and beneath the mask of cream and powder Laurel could detect a suggestion of freckles. Her dark brown hair came to a widow's peak and was combed carelessly back in a long bob.

Not looking at Laurel, she picked up her tennis racket which was leaning against the side of the chair, and the muscles of her forearm tightened as she held it out and sighted along it as though looking to see whether it was warped. "What do you think of him?" she asked.

"Do you mean Mr. Falkoner?" asked Laurel, knowing quite well that Callender meant Mr. Falkoner.

"Yes."

"I really haven't worked with him long enough to say. I've been here only a week."

"Do you know what I think of him?" asked Callender, looking at Laurel out of those no-colored eyes. "I think he's ninety-percent vegetable, with a slight talent for dreaming up tremendous sets."

"Really?" said Laurel.

"Come off it." Callender's voice was as emotionless

as her eyes. She suddenly leaned tensely forward. A
somehow shocking little smile was on her lips. It was
subtle, cunning, and suggestive. "Wouldn't you like to
know what he is? Wouldn't you like to know why he
doesn't give a whoop for woman? Wouldn't you like
to know why he never takes a drink? Wouldn't you like
to know whether he was ever in love? Wouldn't you like
to know what he's looking for?"

"Only mildly," said Laurel.

Rita stood up and went to the window. She stood
with one hand on her hip, the other supporting her
weight against the frame. "Why does he need two
bodyguards?" she asked.

"I thought Jim was his secretary," Laurel said.

"Ha!" said Callender. She strolled to the shelves of
records, idly selected a slender mauve album. Going
to the big white chest, she fitted two records onto the
central pin of the turntable, and started the machine.
The liquid and dreamlike first bars of *The. Afternoon of
a Faun* filled the air of the big, colorful room.

For the first time Laurel had the feeling that there
might be something distasteful lurking beneath the
surface of the lives with which her own had so casually
come into contact. It was a distinctly unpleasant feeling, and Callender seemed to be the touchstone. The
few words she had spoken had brought distorted shadows
into play against a sunny wall in Laurel's mind. Was
she, after all, creating Dickensian simplicities out of
men who were neither simple nor amusing?

She shook her head doggedly.

"Have you met Andy?" asked Callender.

"Oh, yes. He's pleasant, isn't he?"

"He's all right." Callender laughed abruptly. "I
showed him the big city last week. Before you came,
Earl stood me—that is, I stopped past intending to
pick up Earl and take him to the ballet—anyway he

wasn't home, but here was Andy, sitting in this big white chair reading Proust. I don't know why, but I felt sorry for him. So I said, 'Come on, have you ever seen Hollywood?' He hadn't, so we did. All the places. It was a new twist on the rube in the big town. I mean, here's this tiny man who knows Einstein, but he'd never really had himself a time. He was wide-eyed. I don't think he'd ever drunk anything but good wine. I left him at midnight at the Beachcomber's. He was sitting all by himself at a table grinning at the candle flame, with three frozen Daiquiris lined up in front of him."

"Hello, Rita," said Jim's civil voice. He was peering at them past a half-open door at the head of the outside stairs.

"Hello, Jim. How are you?" replied Rita Callender tonelessly.

"Swell. Did Mrs. Lovelace tell you that he won't be home all day?"

"She did."

"Oh." Jim shut the door.

"Wonderful character," said Rita, still in that quiet voice. "I haven't a doubt in the world that his grand-father wore a slew of scalps at his belt."

"That's what Woody thinks."

"Who's Woody?"

"A writer. There are three of us."

"He did that once before," said Rita. "They all of a sudden weren't around any more. I wonder what became of them."

"Do you suppose their bodies could be buried in the garden?" asked Laurel politely.

Rita gave her a look as flat as her voice had been. "I think they stopped being useful to him," she said. She lowered her eyes to the glass figurine on the table beside her chair—a small turquoise nude dancing forever on one toe. "A place for everything and everything in its place," she said, standing up. "I'm going," she announced abruptly. "I'll have some more whisky and a bath. I don't need the bath. Nice to have met you."

The tennis racket dangling from her hand, she moved lithely across the room on her beautiful legs.

The door chimes sounded. Rita continued on her way. Laurel heard the front door creak as she opened it, and then she saw Mrs. Lovelace appear in the narrow arch of the corridor that led back to the kitchen. Her bony hand went to her bosom in a gesture of curious gentility; she seemed to be wearing a look of dismay. Then the look changed, and the change was startling. The nearest Laurel could come to defining the new look on Mrs. Lovelace's face was to label it "malice," but it was an impersonal malice. Turning so abruptly that Laurel could almost hear her bones creak, Mrs. Lovelace went back to the kitchen.

Rita's face appeared around the edge of the archway, just as Jim's had done a week before. Where his big hand had been dark against the plaster of the wall, Rita's was thin and golden and the nails very red. "He didn't bury them in the garden," she said, and disappeared. Laurel heard her throaty voice say, "Hail and farewell, Harvers. He isn't home. I thought you had died or something."

The voice that replied was as rich as fruitcake. "I was just about to ask you who'd robbed *your* grave," it said.

Rita slammed the door.

"These feminine rake-hells are all alike," the fruitcake voice went on to say, and into Laurel's view, moving with a rolling majesty, hove a vast man in a dark suit. His hair, as fine and darkly gold as Laurel's own, was a little long and a trifle disheveled. His pink face, which poured out each side of his white collar in two great jowls, turned slowly toward her, and the look it wore—prim around the tiny moist mouth and hard around the little blue eyes—did not change.

"Good afternoon," he said. "I am Larry Harvers. This—" he made a formal gesture with a small hand that was dimpled, like a baby's—"is my colleague, Robert Nashe."

An angular, dark man, in a light green sport coat and a tan shirt the collar of which was open at the throat just far enough to reveal a small hirsute triangle, came into view. He had very little chin, very thick glasses, and he was sneering.

" 'Do," he said, and looked severely at the window.

Harvers oozed across the soundless carpet to the white chair Rita Callender had just vacated, into which he sank deeply.

Nashe, still looking out the window, went to a red chair and sat easily on its broad arm, his hands in his pockets.

"I'm Laurel Byrd," Laurel said.

"What," demanded Harvers of the air in front of him, "am I sitting on?" He heaved his body to one side and drew Rita's white purse from the depths of the chair. He looked at it, and dropped it to the floor.

Conversation languished.

Laurel stood up, her mouth open to say *I'm sure you will excuse me if I leave to look for some friends of mine,* when the white door going onto the staircase leading down to the terrace opened, admitting Jeff and Woody and a clean rush of air. They were talking animatedly, but stopped on seeing the two strangers.

"This is Mr. Harvers," said Laurel, "and Mr. Nashe. I believe they are writers too. And they used to work for Mr. Falkoner." She appealed to Harvers. "Isn't that right?" she asked, feeling a social smile stretched across her face.

He shook his head heavily from side to side. "It wasn't right," he said. "What you just said was true, of course, but it wasn't right."

Laurel obliquely saw Jeff cast a look of wonder at Woody, who came forward and sat on the low step of the hearth, facing the little group Harvers, Nashe and Laurel made, in their three chairs. Jeff came forward, lighting a cigarette, and half sat on the arm of Laurel's chair.

"Why?" asked Woody. "Why wasn't it right?" He looked innocent, flatteringly interested and somehow very wise.

Harvers, with an effort, thrust his body toward one side of the chair so as to reach into his trousers pocket. To Laurel's infinite astonishment, he drew out a pocket knife with a black bone handle. His plump little hands fingered it for a moment and unsheathed one of the blades, which turned out to be not a blade at all but a corkscrew. "See this?" he asked, and looked from face to face to make sure that they did.

"It's a corkscrew," said Laurel uncertainly.

Harvers fixed his wee eyes on her. "Next to Falkoner," he said, and held the corkscrew up an inch higher, "this is the shortest distance between two points." He snapped the corkscrew back into the handle of the knife and went through the tremendous effort of putting the knife back into his side pocket.

"You mean he's crooked?" asked Jeff, very casually, through a cloud of smoke.

Harvers looked annoyed. "I've said that once, and well. Why should I repeat it badly?"

"Why do you think so?" Woody asked.

"He owes us $500," said Harvers severely.

Jeff leaned forward. "Wait a minute. You mean that he owes you $250, and Mr. Nashe $250."

"You're rather good at addition," said Harvers, a meretricious look of admiration on his face.

Nashe gave a dry laugh. Laurel looked at him. He

was still looking out the window.

"We finished his lousy show three months ago. He suddenly became very hard to find. So we're here to tell him that he pays us, or we haul him into municipal court."

"If you signed a speculative contract, you might as well save yourself the trouble," Woody said.

Harvers looked suspicious.

"And if your contract was anything like ours, that's just what you did sign," Woody added.

Nashe suddenly wasn't looking at the window any more. "Do you have a copy of that contract around?" he asked.

Jeff jumped up, tossing his cigarette into the fireplace. "I'll get mine," he offered. As his footsteps thudded down the staircase, the door chimes sounded once more.

"This seems to be visiting day," said Laurel brightly.

Harvers simply gave her an incredulous stare and then looked moodily at Woody. "How do *you* know so much?" he asked him rudely.

"I'm actually a hundred and twelve years old. I was born on leap year," Woody said gravely.

"Witty, too," Harvers said in the general direction of the doorway leading out to the hall. "There goes Mrs. Lovelace. I often wonder where she mislaid her blood."

There was the sound of a woman's voice in the hall, speaking too softly for Laurel to distinguish the words. But she heard Mrs. Lovelace say guardedly, "Oh, I'm sure he'd never forgive me if you left. If you wouldn't mind *waiting*—"

Laurel heard the other woman's voice then. "I'll wait," she said, and came through the doorway.

Mrs. Lovelace hovered uncertainly in the background for a moment, and then melted into the dark little corridor leading back to her kitchen.

The blond woman who came into the room walked

with the calm assurance of a welcome. She wore a suit
of muted blue, created by Adrian for someone like herself, five sables, and a small and exquisite hat of exactly
the same blue as the suit. One splendid diamond blazed
beside a platinum wedding band as she raised her hand
to loosen the furs at her throat. Her nails were pale
pink.

Harvers hauled himself to his feet.

"Please go right on with your conversation," she said
in a ladylike voice. "I wouldn't interrupt an artistic
discussion for the world."

She passed the three of them with a vague, bright
smile, and Laurel noticed her face for the first time. She
had large, shallow blue eyes—the heavy lids made them
look weary, her mascara made them look a little hard.
Her nose was small and perfect, and her mouth was
painted on carefully with a pleasing red. It was hard
to tell its real shape, but Laurel suspected that beneath
those rich alien curves it was ungenerous. She walked
with small, neat steps to a red chair at the far end of
the room, sat down, opened her purse and drew out a
golden flat case from which she took a cigarette, placing
it deftly between her lips. Before she could light it,
Woody was there with a match.

Laurel caught a glimpse of those blue eyes looking
up at him. She exhaled. She said, "Thank you so
much," in a voice which didn't thank him at all, but
merely accepted his gesture as her due, and drew a maga-
zine from the table beside her chair, spreading it wide.
It was Vogue. The woman on the cover had on a hat
exactly like her own.   •

Jeff strolled into the room then with his contract;
he handed it to Harvers, and saw the woman in blue at
the far end of the room. He stared at her, and Laurel
realized that their eyes were the same color. Abstractly,
one long hand went to his tie and straightened it; the

other went up and passed over the well-disciplined waves of his dark hair. He walked to Laurel's chair and, still looking at the woman in blue, whispered, "Who is that?"

"I don't know," Laurel whispered back, a little amazed at his reaction. "She strolled in and said something polite about not interrupting, and went over there and sat down."

Jeff nodded his thanks, and went down the long room to the lady in blue.

Laurel turned to watch him. He gave his youthful half-bow which always made Laurel think of a little boy in dancing school, and she heard him say, "May I introduce myself? My name's Jefferson Prince."

Her voice ripe with the wise amusement of an older woman for the gallantry of a younger man, the lady in blue said, "And mine's Denise Morrissey."

"It's the same blooming contract," Harvers announced harshly, looking up from the long sheet of paper on his shallow lap. "Two hundred and fifty bucks when the play's finished, a half interest in the show split among you. Oh, that heel, that louse!" He looked down at the contract. "Punk title," he commented, in a perfectly easy tone. *"That Was Yesterday*. Pee-yew." His voice went nasty again. "It's a damned good thing he doesn't eat meat. He'd go in for the big-time stuff. Murder, arson and bank robbery. Not just rooking writers still in diapers!"

Laurel heard them coming. Or rather, she heard Tom's heavy tread on the outer stairs leading down to the terrace. Plainly oblivious, Jeff was saying to Denise Morrissey, "—and Woody's been everywhere twice and loves it. He's eaten fried bumblebees; he saw an incredibly rich Oriental tin magnate signal his henchmen to murder some political enemies while they were eating a dinner in their honor; and next he's going to Martinique to—"

The white door next to the view window opened. Jim came in first, on noiseless bare feet, his splendid torso silhouetted against the late afternoon. "Hello, Harvers. Hello, Nashe."

"Hello, Atlas," said Harvers, his eyes as cold as aquamarines. "Developed any new muscles lately?"

"A few," said Jim equably.

"So have I," said Tom, and grinned.

"Were you waiting for Mr. Falkoner?" asked Jim.

"Not were," corrected Harvers. "*We are*."

"You were," said Tom, still grinning.

Jim turned his head toward Tom without looking at him. "Shut up," he said. And to Harvers: "He's gone for the day. He won't be home much before midnight."

Ignoring Jim, Harvers turned his great head toward Nashe. "You owe me fifty cents." To Woody: "I bet him all my worldly wealth that something very like this would happen." He looked thoughtfully at nothing, and then lifted his shoulder in a slight shrug. "Well—" Placing both cherubic hands on the arms of the chair, he just managed to get himself into a horizontal position. Looking at Jim, and at Tom, and then at Jim again, his tiny mouth thinned in contempt. "I see now where you two come in," he said softly. "Come on, Nashe."

"I think—" began Nashe.

"We'll think later," said Harvers. He trundled to the doorway with Nashe at his heels, ridiculous and colorful and small, and wearing his sneer again.

In the archway Harvers turned for a moment. He surveyed them with elaborate pity. "You've seen the handwriting on the wall, kiddies," he said. "It spells 'skunk.'" And he rolled out.

"I've done Europe, of course," Denise was saying to Jeff, and Laurel had the feeling that she was firmly and deliberately removing herself from the unpleasantness at the other end of the room. "England was boiled beef and Naples was grand. But somehow I've never had time for the out-of-the-way corners. . . ."

Jim and Tom noticed her for the first time. "Hello, Mrs. Morrissey," they said, almost in a duet.

She peered around Jeff's slender attentiveness. "Hello, Jim, Tom." She knows when to be regal, Laurel thought cattily.

"When didja get back?" asked Tom.

"Today." She rose. "Well, I think I'll go on. Tell Mr. Falkoner I stopped by, and that I want very much· to see him, will you, please?"

"I sure will," said Tom.

Mrs. Morrissey gave Jeff her hand—just enough of it, thought Laurel—and then passed by Laurel's chair with that vague, bright smile, apparently quite unconscious of the fact that Jeff was at her heels.

The door chimes sounded and went on sounding. Jim and Tom looked at each other, and Tom turned and went out the white door and down the outer stairs again. Jim went across the room and out the archway into the hall.

"I left my purse, I'm afraid," said a husky voice a moment later, and then Rita was in the room. She came in briskly, and stopped dead a few paces from Denise. She looked at her for a long moment and then rushed forward. Both women were suddenly holding each other's hands.

Rita's smile was vivid and friendly and quite transformed the sullen, ordinary face. "Darling!" she caroled. "How terrible you look!"

Denise's smile was far sweeter than Rita's. "Darling, I know! But there was that plane wreck—you read about it in the papers—oh, no, you don't read them, but there *was*. So at the last moment my knees went weak and **so I took the streamliner** and I *never* sleep on trains.

So I mean two haggard nights listening to wheels, and I mean I've got into the habit. I'm not sleepy, not a bit, just exhausted. . . ."

They dropped each other's hands and, still smiling, went to the two white chairs which faced each other across the width of the hearth. The black mouth of the fireplace yawned emptily between them.

"Who did you see, how are the plays? I'm dying to know," Rita chanted.

Denise settled back in her chair, exactly as though she would rather be there than any other place on earth. She drew a cigarette from her purse, and Jeff, who had been hovering a little behind her chair, held out a lighted match. Rita leaned a little forward, her arms cocked awkwardly, her hands on her bare golden knees, and repeated, "You look *terrible!* You must have had a marvelous time!"

"Marvelous," agreed Denise, expelling smoke. "New York is always marvelous and a little boring at the same time just because there is so *much.* I saw Bunny Hodge, and she's gained weight. The hips, of course, being Bunny, and her new husband's adorable, but absolutely *no* chin!"

Laurel sat watching them, and felt a small smile on her mouth. She watched them knowing that neither woman was necessarily the fool she sounded, knowing they were of a certain scarcely definable social group, a group where there was always a little too much money and never quite enough to occupy the minds of its women.

They have to behave like that, she thought. *It's part of the pattern they belong to.*

"—sleep," Denise was saying. "This woman I met simply thinks of black—everything black—the black swan on the black lake, and no moon. . . . But it doesn't work for me. A dress or someone's face pops into the picture." With sweet sympathy in her voice, she added, "But you know how *that* is—"

Rita's smile left her.

Denise smiled at Rita. "Have you two met?" she asked.

Rita's eyes went from the crown of Jeff's head to the soles of his feet. She shook her head.

"Miss Callender—Mr. Prince," said Denise, using one hand vaguely.

Jeff turned swiftly. "And this is Miss Byrd and Mr. Cornell."

Everyone murmured, and there was a pause. Rita looked at Denise rather as though she might be going to say, *Darling, you look terrible!* again, but it was Jeff who spoke. Looking down at Denise protectively, he said, "Laurel, what about that sleeping pill André gave you?"

"Well," said Laurel, "it put me to sleep."

Denise looked at her mildly. *"Did* it, my dear?" She looked up at Jeff, and for the first time Laurel noticed that there were pale purple circles under her eyes. Closer to forty than thirty, she decided.

"Do get me one," Denise said to Jeff.

He was out of the room almost before she stopped speaking.

"André's not up there, you know," Laurel called after him. "He went on another mysterious jaunt today."

"I'll rummage," Jeff's voice called back, and his feet beat a muffled tattoo on the narrow staircase that curved up to the tower room.

"We'll have dinner together," Rita was saying to Denise. "We'll stop at my place and I'll change. The Beachcomber's. I haven't been there for over a week."

"I can't, dear, really I can't," Denise began.

But Rita countered: "But we have so much to *say* to each other!"

For just a flicker of an instant Laurel caught a look between them—a vacant little look—and knew exactly what Rita was doing. She was getting Denise away before Falkoner might return and find her there, for whatever she might mean to him.

It was precisely twenty-four hours later that she learned about the arsenic.

Chapter Four
Much Worse Than Someone Ugly

Thursday, they learned, was Mrs. Lovelace's day off. Laurel, Jeff and Woody were in the Red Room, hard at work on the changes Falkoner had spilled out that morning before he left for the beach. There was a tapping on the door.

"Come in, by all means," called Jeff, who was doing a turn at the typewriter.

The door opened hesitantly, and Mrs. Lovelace entered with a curious, sidling walk. Her crone-like face was relieved of some of its pallor by two rich patches of rouge set neatly in the hollows below her cheekbones. She was pulling on a pair of white cotton gloves.

"I'm going now," she told them, in her unmodulated voice which never seemed to have to stop for breath. "I always go about this time, I'll be back in the morning, there's plenty for dinner in the icebox. . . . I don't know whether Mr. Falkoner plans to eat at home or out. . . . Sometimes he does one and sometimes he does the other. . . . Jim fixes dinner. There's plenty of food in the icebox." She settled her hat more firmly on her head. It was a ladylike hat with roses. She coughed into one white glove.

"Why did you give me that pamphlet with my orange juice the first morning we came here, Mrs. Lovelace?" asked Woody, his head cocked to one side.

Mrs. Lovelace looked straight at him out of her flat eyes. "We spread what light we can," she said.

Woody raised his eyebrows. "Who's we?"

"I am a member of the Temple of Ultimate Revelation," she said simply.

54

"Oh," said Woody.

"I do wish you'd attend our services one Sunday. The Reverend Bluefeather would make you see. Oh, I know there's a great many people who joke about her, but they are blind. They say she is a showman—I say, isn't it curious that she should have been blessed with that wonderful speaking voice and platform manner? It was, of course, part of His plan."

She gave them a weak smile, the first Laurel had ever seen on her face. It had in it both triumph and superiority. She tiptoed out.

Curiously, even Jeff did not wisecrack.

"The person with a talisman," said Woody, "is one of the miracles. I would rather have a rabbit's foot that I believed in than the most scrupulous agnosticism possible."

"Are you an agnostic then?" asked Laurel.

"I," said Woody, "am a stomach wandering through life."

"Look," said Jeff, in his most reasonable manner, "why don't we go down to Hollywood for dinner?" He glanced at the litter of crumpled sheets around the desk. "This place looks like a goat's nest. And we haven't been out of this room except to eat and sleep for a hundred years."

"What would Falkoner—?" began Laurel, almost timidly.

"Listen," said Jeff, standing up abruptly. "He doesn't own us. And if what Harvers said is true, he doesn't intend to pay us. I want to go to Don the Beachcomber's and dunk myself in the fleshpots."

"I'm hungry," said Woody. "Listen, my stomach is rumbling."

"Look, peanut," Jeff said to Laurel, very matter-of-factly, "you get into something devastating, we'll shave and we'll meet you upstairs in fifteen minutes."

"You're devastating as you are," said Woody hurriedly, with an anxious look in his eyes. "Just powder your nose and let it go at that."

Laurel was the first one upstairs. She was lighting a cigarette, hoping that Falkoner wouldn't come in, when André pattered down the stairs leading to his tower room.

"We haven't seen much of you lately," she said.

"I've been looking for a place to live. I'm going to work at Cal Tech soon. It's very hard to find a place near a university." He hesitated, and then said, "I wonder, did you find yourself in need of more phenobarbital? I've looked everywhere, but I can't seem to find the box. Of course, I may have lost—"

As he spoke, Laurel's eyes went to the mantel where she had seen Jeff lay the box after offering it to Denise Morrissey. It was still there, small and tan and scarcely noticeable, beside the bright red leather box which held the matches for the fireplace. She pointed. "There it is. Jeff borrowed one for a lady who couldn't sleep. He fell in love with her at first sight, and that was all he could do for her at the moment."

Andy went hesitantly over and reached up for the box. He looked at the lid as though he were glad to have it back again, and then turned abruptly and went upstairs to his room.

Jeff and Woody came up then. "I don't think André liked your helping yourself to his pills," she said.

"Oh, well," replied Jeff.

They went gaily to the front door. Jeff flung the door blithely open and they found themselves face to face with a small, neat, gray-haired man who had just put his finger to the bell.

"How do you do?" he said, in a modest, quiet voice. "I am Dr. Day. I should like to have a word with the young man who gave Mrs. Morrissey a sleeping capsule yesterday."

Jeff looked vaguely startled. "I am he," he said formally. "Won't you come in?"

"Thank you," said Dr. Day. He ran his hand back over his crisp hair in lieu of removing a hat, and preceded them into the living-room.

"This is a rather delicate situation," he confessed. "But in these cases a doctor has a duty not only to his patient, but to the state as well. And I've seen one or two rather ghastly errors made by pharmacists in my time." He looked about the room. "May I sit down?" he asked.

"Oh, yes. Do," said Laurel, wondering with an uneasiness in the pit of her stomach what was coming next.

"You mean there was something wrong with the capsule?" asked Woody.

"I believe that it may have contained a fatal dose of arsenic," Dr. Day said in an astoundingly everyday tone.

"But that's impossible!" Jeff protested. "Laurel took one of them a week ago, and it didn't hurt her in the least!" He turned to Laurel. "Did it?"

"No," Laurel confirmed, dazed. "No, not in the least."

"Please," pleaded Woody, putting one hand on his stomach as though commanding it to behave. "What happened?"

Sitting straight in one of the white chairs, his hands relaxed on its arm, Dr. Day explained. "Mrs. Morrissey and I both live at The Towers, which probably saved her life. Last night the man at the switchboard rang me at ten-thirty. Mrs. Morrissey, it seems, had phoned him to get a doctor, that she was ill. He had seen me come in a few minutes before, and so called me.

"Her symptoms—vomiting and acute intestinal discomfort—did not at once give me the notion that poison was the cause, although it was among the possibilities that I considered; all diagnosis is a process of elimination,

as you probably know. I questioned her closely about
what she had eaten and drunk during the twelve hours
preceding the attack. She mentioned the sleeping capsule you gave her, Mr. Prince, and I made a mental note
of it. To brief the matter, my very tentative diagnosis
of poison was confirmed an hour ago by the laboratory
to which I took the sample of the vomitus for analysis.
They estimated that she had ingested about one hundred
milligrams of arsenic trioxide."

He looked mildly at their stunned faces. "So I should
like very much to take that box of capsules to the same
laboratory for chemical analysis; I cannot overlook the
fact that the sleeping capsule she took is one of the possible sources of the poison."

Jeff stood up abruptly and went out into the hall.
"Andy!" they heard him call. "Bring down that box of
sleeping stuff! It's full of arsenic!"

André's shocked little cry came faintly down the rear
stairs. In a moment there was a swift patter of feet, and
in another moment Jeff and André came into the room
together.

André had the box in his hand and went directly
to Dr. Day. "This is the box," he said. "But I don't
understand. I don't understand at all. This is phenobarbital."

"Have you taken any yourself?" asked the doctor, a
quick shadow of anxiety in his tone.

André shook his head. "Not for several days. But
I have certainly used capsules from this box, and—" he
gave a very Gallic shrug—"here I am."

The doctor smiled a little. He stood up. "Well, we'll
see. It does look rather as though I have been barking
up the wrong tree, but I am sure you can all see that
I have done the only sensible thing in the circumstances."

"But who?" asked André, still rather excited. "Who,
who, who has been poisoned with my sleeping pills?"

"A Mrs. Morrissey. You know her?"

"I met her a month or so ago, before she left for the East. A charming woman. I am—" He made a little queer gesture. "It is much worse than had it been someone old and ugly." He turned his smile on and off.

All the time he was speaking, Laurel watched him. She could not tell exactly why, but she was deeply sure that he was acting, and rather well.

When Dr. Day had gone, André went to the window and stood looking out at the garden where night was thickening. Then he turned and ran one small hand through his shock of black hair. Laurel saw that he was trembling. And when he spoke, she knew why he had been acting.

"A rather unpleasant thought occurred to me while the doctor was talking," he said. "Do you know what it is?" Laurel shook her head but he didn't see her do it. He was looking at the floor, his fine black brows drawn together in a slight frown. "If there is arsenic in those capsules, someone has tried to kill me."

CHAPTER FIVE
TWO EMPTY COTS

"WHAT's that?" asked a voice, and they turned to find Falkoner standing very still, watching them with his yachting cap tilted to one side, his eyes pale and hard and fixed immovably on André.

"I said," repeated André, "that someone may be trying to kill me."

Falkoner shook his head from side to side, never taking his eyes from André. "No one's trying to kill you, fellow," he said. He said it slowly, emphatically.

"I hope not," said André, and turned his grin on and off.

Falkoner continued on his way into the room, stopping as usual at the hearth. Standing on one solid leg, his back to them, he removed the square-toed shoe from the other foot, and shook sand from it into the cold fireplace.

"What's all this about?" he asked with irritable carelessness.

"Your friend Mrs. Morrissey seems to have picked up some poison somewhere or other," said Jeff. "The doctor who took care of her suspected the sleeping capsule I gave her from André's little box."

Falkoner pivoted on his stockinged foot. "She was perfectly all right when I phoned her at nine last night!"

"It didn't hit her until ten, the doctor says," Jeff explained.

Falkoner slid his foot into his shoe and stamped it on. "I'll look into this!" he said loudly, authoritatively.

He went with heavy swiftness out of the room, turning in the round hall. "Where do you three think you're going?"

"To dinner," Woody said. "Mrs. Lovelace has left some perfectly yummy things in the icebox, but we're too hungry to wait."

"O. K.," said Falkoner. "O. K. You can take my car if you want."

"Thanks. Jeff's car will do," Woody replied.

"Suit yourself," said Falkoner. "Don't be late. We've got a lot to do tomorrow. I got a swell new idea while I was swimming."

"I should think the water would have been too cold for anything but freezing to death," commented Jeff, with one eyebrow raised very high.

"People humor their bodies too much," Falkoner said. "They eat the wrong things and drink the wrong things and don't get enough sun. But you'll do what you please, you and André. You and your brains." He gave a short laugh, turned and strode heavily down the narrow corridor to the booth where the upstairs phone was hidden.

"Would you like to join us for dinner?" Woody asked André.

"No, thank you. I have some things to do." They left him staring out the window. From the garden below came the sudden wild barking of the dogs.

As they went out the front door they heard Falkoner's voice booming hollowly from the telephone booth. "—three dozen gardenias," he was commanding. "Fix them the way you did the last time. Use long-stemmed ones and wire them into a bouquet. I want something slightly on the quaint side, and ladylike. And send them to—"

They went to the Beachcomber's. The proprietor, a small man, Shakespeareanly bald and wearing a gorgeous lei and a shabby white suit, permitted them a table near the door. The frequent draft was bad but the food was wonderful. Laurel wondered at which table André had sat smiling at his Daiquiris, surrounded by the thick transplanted atmosphere which gradually changed the draft to trade winds but could not strip the men of their checked coats nor the women of their high-breasted and suave Hollywood voluptuousness.

"I think," said Woody, as he paid the check, refusing their money in exactly the right fashion, "that I should like to see Ruth De Lisle. I think you might like it too."

They reached the entrance to the De Lisle's house by many shallow steps arranged in three levels. On each level a rectangular basin held still, black water, and by day would reflect the dark cedar trees planted at precise intervals at either side of the steps. "Just like the public library," marveled Laurel dryly.

The front door was opened abruptly by a stocky man in a dark suit. He had small, wicked black eyes which flitted across their faces carelessly. His voice was careless too, and very British. Taking Woody's hand briefly and punctiliously in his own, he said with no emotion whatever, "Nice to see you again. Veddy nice. Come inside."

The living-room was big and easy and full of deep rich colors. The old grand piano, the Italian triptych, the pale Utrillo above the olive-green sofa had never been assembled by any decorator. Seeing the room you knew that Harold and Ruth De Lisle had lived for a long time with their furniture and would never be divorced from it by the artistic convictions of any professional dresser of rooms.

"What will you drink?" asked Harold.

They had just decided on Scotch and soda when Laurel heard the front door open, and then Ruth De Lisle was there, clasping Woody in a statuesque embrace. Harold De Lisle removed her mink coat and left the room with it cascading richly down over one arm.

She was one of those rare women who, although dressed very smartly, have a body and not a figure. Her long black gown had just a hint of a train which endowed her with a fluid grace when she moved, and which, when she was seated, made a puddle of dull black beside her high-arched slender feet. Her hair fascinated Laurel. It was shining chestnut, wound about her head in a coil—a coiffure which Ruth De Lisle was certainly clever enough to know accented the aquilinity of her nose. She was also clever enough to know, Laurel decided, that since her nose was aquiline, she might as well flaunt the fact. The proud fine nose was belied by her smile—a beautiful, real smile full of prominent white teeth. Like most women, she undoubtedly loved the sound of her own voice, but hers was a voice to love. A clear voice, coming from the back of the throat. An American voice. Laurel found her eyes the most engaging part of her face; they were accented with green eye shadow which was frankly eye shadow, put on to look well at twenty paces. She wore dangling garnet earrings which were heirlooms, and she smoked her cigarette in one of those long black holders which filter out most of the nicotine.

When Woody began talking about the house on the hill, Ruth De Lisle leaned forward and interrupted him. "You don't mean that you're *living* there!"

"Yes, all of us."

Ruth leaned back in her chair again, but Laurel was sure she did not hear another word that Woody said.

It was when Harold De Lisle was standing in front of her, offering down a tall plain crystal glass full of clear tinkling amber, that Laurel learned why Woody had chosen this particular night to make this particular visit.

"You know Denise Morrissey, don't you?" he asked, looking innocently out at Ruth over the rim of his glass.

"Darling, I've known her forever. Actually. We went to the same high school in Pomona. She was Denise Hooper then. One of those blond pale little girls."

"Do you think that she would be likely to try to commit suicide?" asked Woody.

There was a snort. Laurel looked over at the low rocking chair, a little apart from the group, where Harold De Lisle was sitting with his Scotch and soda. He was dabbing at his tie with a blindingly white handkerchief.

"Darling. Your *new* tie," said Ruth. She turned back to Woody. "Whatever put such an idea into your head?"

"Arsenic did," said Woody sagely. "You see, she's full of arsenic."

"Arsenic?" repeated Ruth, her green eyes more prominent than ever.

"Arsenic," repeated Woody.

Ruth jumped up. "I must call her," she said over her shoulder, and vanished into another room.

"The veddy supposition that Denise Morrissey took arsenic," said Harold De Lisle solemnly, "turns this room and all of you into something out of dream. Do you like my Utrillo?"

They talked about Utrillo.

In a little while Ruth came back. "Well, she's feeling much better. From what she told me the reaction was something like what I had the time I drank too much cheap red wine in Italy—remember, Harold? The nurse who took care of her today suggested champagne, because she can only take liquids and hates milk. She can't dream where she got it. The arsenic, I mean."

"Did she tell you about the sleeping capsule?" asked Woody.

"Yes. And from I've gathered she's more or less in favor of the theory that some pharmacist or other reached for the wrong bottle when he made up the capsules.

And that's actually my guess because she had lunch on the train and only a chicken sandwich, and anyway she thinks that's much too early. She ate dinner at the Beachcomber's with Rita, the same food exactly, and Rita's fine. Then of course she had a tiny glass of sherry here at four—just before she met you at Earl's. ∴ . ."

There was a small stillness in the room.

"And my wife," said Harold De Lisle, "serves poisoned sherry only on very special occasions."

An ember popped in the fireplace across the room where small flames were diminishing.

"What are she and Falkoner to each other?" Woody asked.

"I don't know," said Ruth. "I truly don't know. She is a trifle awed by his talent, of course."

"Oh, good heavens!" said Harold De Lisle. They all looked at him. His little eyes were wicked again, and his face seemed red. "I saw a picture he did the sets for—what was the name?—it was a musical. Horrible! This great white thing with tiers and they all revolved and people danced and sang. I have rarely suffered such boredom and such extreme embarrassment."

Ruth was nodding. "Earl seems rather to think that the bigger anything is, the better," she murmured. "He was born in Texas, I believe," she added vaguely.

"How long have he and Denise known each other?" asked Woody.

"Oh, years and years. He did some things for her husband, Joel Morrissey. A producer. Joel died several years ago. He wouldn't take time out to go to the hospital and his appendix burst on the set one day."

"Is she in love with Falkoner? Is he in love with her?" Woody prodded.

Ruth shook her head. She was looking vaguely at the embers in the fireplace. "I really don't know. It's always such a mistake to assume that blond people are without passion, but I truly think that Denise was in love for the first and last time when she was nineteen years old."

"And Falkoner?"

Ruth De Lisle didn't answer.

"Love," said Harold De Lisle, "is a bit of a habit, you know. I believe that Falkoner never formed the habit. That's all."

There was another little silence.

"I may, of course, be mistaken," said Harold De Lisle.

"How about Rita Callender? Where does she come into the picture?" asked Woody.

"You know how you come across the same mentality in different bodies?" Harold De Lisle asked Woody. "I've met Callender before. Twice in London society, once singing in a bar in Budapest, several times in America. People like that create situations and then milk them of every drop of sensation. I suspect that Callender prefers pain. She can become attached to a man only if he can hurt her. Falkoner is her natural meat. The moment he showed himself impervious to her mild desire for a flirtation, she was lashed to him by bonds as strong as real love."

"You're very literate, darling," said Ruth with genuine pride.

Harold De Lisle bristled a little. "I know the Callender," he said brusquely.

"Why does Falkoner have two bodyguards?" asked Laurel, deciding that since questions being asked, she might as well ask one herself.

With the air of concluding a discussion no longer interesting, Ruth stated firmly, "Earl is feudal. Definitely feudal. He likes being the king at his own board; he likes having vassals around him. I never see his feet without thinking of square-toed suits of fourteenth-century armor."

Harold De Lisle looked down into his glass. He tipped it gently so that the cube of ice clunked against its side with a subdued sound. "It's odd that you should have that feeling about him, my dear, disliking him as you do," he said to his glass. He looked up at them and his eyes were dull. "My wife has a veddy decided passion for all things medieval," he added.

Ruth De Lisle suddenly held out her empty glass. "I should very much like another drink, my dear," she said. "I think we all do."

"Of course. Stupid of me," murmured Harold, on his feet immediately. He gathered up the glasses and left the room.

Ruth De Lisle leaned toward Woody. "Listen," she whispered. "Get away from that house, and get away from Falkoner. I mean it. I know what I am talking about."

"Yours will be mostly soda, Ruth," called Harold from the other room. "You did have that sherry this afternoon, you know. . . ."

"Whatever you say, dear," Ruth answered brightly.

The house was dark when they returned to it. They walked across the bridge in the bright cold moonlight, and there was lateness in the sound of their footsteps. Woody used the key which Falkoner had given him early in the week, and the heavy door swung in silently.

Jeff went to the head of the stairs leading down to their bedrooms and snapped the switch that turned on the light in the lower hall. They stood for a moment there in the darkness, with the downstairs light overflowing through the horizontals of the balustrade around the stair well.

Woody's voice was grave as he said, "I think we'd better be quite clear in our heads when we analyze the writing on the wall, and I think we should analyze it before we see Falkoner again." He looked over his shoulder at the dark arch that led to the living-room. "Shall we meet in the garden before breakfast?"

Laurel set the alarm of her small clock for 7:30. As she turned the projecting button on the back of the clock until the tiny metal finger on the clock's face pointed to the hour at which she would begin a new day, she experienced a sudden feeling of comfort. The sense of strangeness and uneasiness which had been with her almost constantly for the past week evaporated. Quite conscious that she was indulging in the most sentimental sort of pathetic fallacy, she felt for a moment that the little clock's face was the face of a very old friend, who had patiently substituted for her own will-power for four long years, awaking her for classes with unflagging faithfulness. She set it down on the bedside table and there was a solid thump as its metal touched the white wood, and it was only a clock after all. But its tiny ticking in the darkness was soothing, and she felt the muscles of her face relax in almost a smile as she sank into the pleasing bog of sleep.

Fuddled with sleep she awoke and shut off the alarm. The room was very cold, and the cold was intensified by the blue walls, with the white furniture standing out hard against them. Shivering, she raced to the window and closed it, seeing as she did so that the hills to the west were rosy gilt from the newly risen sun. She dressed hurriedly, racing toward the final comfort of her camel's-hair coat, which she wore while she cleaned her teeth and combed her hair. Her lipstick was hard in its golden tube; she hurriedly painted her mouth and gladly left her room for the garden. She heard the alarm in Jeff's and Woody's room begin to sound as she passed out of the house through the French window opening onto the cement terrace, which the sun would not touch until afternoon. She decently averted her eyes as she passed the three cots.

The shadow of the house stopped sharp and blue on the sloping lawn of the garden below the terrace; beyond it the grass was very green and bright with dew. Some blackbirds wearing blue irradiance on their feathers were hurrying with swift aimlessness about the lawn, moving their heads with unnecessary bird-like motions as they walked. Laurel thought of their larger and more terrible ancestors who in the days before gas chambers had dined fiercely on what remained on English gibbets when hangman and spectators had gone away.

The thought did not match the sunlight about her. Not yet quite awake, she walked to a neatly pruned bush and stood for a long time examining the casual perfection of a coral-colored rose halfway between bud and full flower. But a persistent morbidity seemed to be with her this morning, for in a moment her mind was chiming the lines:

I sometimes think that never blows so red
The rose as where some buried Caesar bled. . .

She turned back to the house, which had imperceptibly withdrawn its shadow while she had watched the black-birds and the flower.

She was conscious that there had been a slight pale warmth to the early sun when she stepped again into the shadow of the house. Reaching the top of the flat steps leading from the garden to the terrace she found herself facing the three cots below the outer staircase. The two outer cots were empty. Falkoner was still in his.

He was lying on his back, his head tilted a little forward on the pillow. The sole of one bare foot protruded starkly from the ugly tan of the blankets. One hand hung down, its back resting on the cement beside the bed. His eyes were looking straight at her. Their

iciness had melted at last into a look far less pleasant—
the wet, cold look of death.

She stood watching him with the stupid intenseness
with which she had looked at the rose. Then every
inch of her awoke, and she heard her own scream knife
across the morning air, killing the tentative chirpings
of the blackbirds in the sunlit garden below.

CHAPTER SIX

THE MOST SLY AND CRUEL WEAPON

As TUCK reached the outer door of the office of the Homicide Squad, he heard his own name mentioned.

"If Tuck is going to get all the genteel cases, Gufferty," Brigit Estees' deep warm voice was saying, "why, then I want to go along with."

"Genteel? What's genteel about murder?"

"What I mean," pursued Brigit's voice, "if you've decided he's a white blackbird, why, so am I, on account of wearing a skirt instead of pants. So I want to go along with."

"*Are you accusing me of favoritism?*" asked Gufferty of everyone in the Los Angeles City Hall.

"Lord love you, no," said Brigit mildly. "But maybe you know a good man when you see one, and maybe I do too. So how about it?"

"No," said Gufferty in his cross, furry voice.

At this moment Tuck became aware of the fact that he was eavesdropping, more out of force of habit than because he cared greatly what the Chief of the Homicide Squad and its sole woman member might think of him. He opened the door.

Gufferty looked out balefully from beyond Brigit's red head. "Oh," he said, "you."

"Me. Anything new? Oh, the boys are at the jail working over Hypo Bob. He supplied the dope, all right."

"*You* caught Hypo Bob, so why aren't you at the jail too?"

Tuck looked intently at Gufferty's bald spot, with its tonsure of graying hair. "I don't like force as a means of getting at the truth. I can't win the boys over to my private beliefs."

"*There's no rubber hoses used in this department!*" announced Gufferty. "And when there is," he added uncomfortably, "it's only when necessary. Go on home."

"Hello, Tuck," said Brigit.

"Hello, Estees," said Tuck, and turned to open the door.

The phone rang. Gufferty grabbed the receiver and said, "Homicide Squad Gufferty speakin'!"

Tuck opened the door.

"So long," said Brigit.

"So long," said Tuck.

"*Wait!*" yelled Gufferty. He drew a scratch-pad toward him across the polished surface of his desk, and jotted rapidly. He listened, nodding. "Right." He hung up the receiver.

"So you don't go home after all, Tuck. You go—" he glanced at the·pad, tore off the sheet and handed it out across the desk—"to 310 Ridgetop Drive. There's a Hollywood gent named Earl Falkoner lying in bed dead, and he's probably been poisoned."

Brigit let out a long, masculine, envious whistle.

"Estees, you'll go along with," said Gufferty crossly.

She bounced to her feet, and had her Knox hat on before she reached Tuck's side.

"I'll get ahold of the medical examiner. He and one of the fingerprint boys'll reach the place about the same time you do," Gufferty planned.

They started out the door. "Oh, and Estees," called Gufferty, "this is definitely very genteel, because the place is full of writers."

"God love you," said Brigit. "You're a white man."

Gufferty scowled.

A Lieutenant Threep passed them as they went down the echoing marble hall. The knuckles of his right hand were bandaged. In a moment they heard Gufferty. *"How often do I have to tell you that I don't like force as a means of getting at the truth?"* he was saying.

"It's a beautiful day to die on," said Brigit tentatively as their black sedan turned and went from north Broadway onto Sunset Boulevard.

Tuck parked two inches from the rear bumper of a black-and-white police car, in front of a white stucco house with a tower. Brigit's quivering intentness to get to the job ahead emphasized for him the fact that his own body was full of the dregs of the weariness of last night's long and ugly job. Like a starving man filling his stomach with an imagined feast, he decided gravely and carefully that what he wanted more than anything was to be in a hot bath with a pot of coffee at his elbow and some good, strong music to listen to. Sibelius would be best, he thought, as he slammed the car door. Full of ice and power. And beauty.

As he crossed the bridge which led to the front door of the imitation castle, he raised his tired eyes to the midmorning sky. It was a wide blue sky relieved by a streak of marbled cloud above the Sierras. As Brigit had said, it was a beautiful day to die on. No, wait. He looked down at Brigit, striding capably beside him on her size-eight oxfords. "Did you say it was a beautiful day to die on?"

"Yes."

"You meant *too* beautiful a day to die on, didn't you?"

"No. I meant it was a beautiful day to die on."

Morbid, thought Tuck morbidly, and pushed his forefinger against the doorbell.

The door was opened by a burly young and navy-blue-serge-and-black-leather policeman, alert and smiling. Before Tuck was completely in the house, he thrust a list into Tuck's hand—a neatly written column of names and addresses.

"Officer Scudder reporting, sir. I arrived at three minutes after nine, exposed my shield and held everyone for questioning. I notified headquarters, giving a brief outline of the case, which is: The dead man is named Earl Falkoner. He was found dead in his bed this morning by Laurel Byrd—" he politely indicated the first name on his list—"who is one of three writers living here at the present. The body is on a—I guess you'd call it a sort of a balcony—at the rear of the house. That is where the dead man habitually slept, so there's nothing funny there. I have prevented anyone from seeing or touching the body. No unauthorized persons have attempted to enter the house. I have kept the witnesses, if you can call them that, separate by seating them at intervals around the living-room, my partner and I then watching them like hawks. They have had no conversation with one another since my arrival. I have given the body only a cursory examination, as I did not want to disturb it before you got to see it. There are no wounds or blood."

Yearning to say, *No blood, huh? What kind of an officer do you think you are?* Tuck nodded his head gravely, and allowed Scudder to lead him to the body. They passed from the entrance hall through a room full of frightened and uncomfortable-looking people proctored by an officer as alert as Scudder. Tuck wondered idly how long it would take him to undo Scudder's good work and get them into a mood for confidences.

At the bottom of an outer flight of steps, Scudder veered abruptly to the left, went three steps, and stopped.

The dead man stared out of the shadow below the stairs at the sunny day; the shadow stopped sharply at his ankle, so that one bare foot was tan in the sun, the rest of him dead in the shadow.

"A fine physical specimen," commented Scudder approvingly.

Tuck noticed the degree of rigor and estimated that the fine physical specimen had been dead for at least ten hours. There was no wound or blood; the skin around the mouth was normal, so the poison, if poison it was, had not been caustic.

"What makes you think it's poison?" he asked Scudder, covering the body with the bedclothes.

Scudder waved a hand up at the living-room. "They all say so," he said.

Tuck looked up and sighed. That roomful of theys, all needing to be cleansed of fear and horror and stiffness. And among them, perhaps, a hand with no mark upon it which had nevertheless wielded for an unknown reason the most sly and cruel weapon of them all.

"You've done a fine job, Scudder," he said. "No need to keep you any longer."

"Right, sir."

Somehow Tuck had known that he would say, "Right, sir."

"What do I do?" asked Brigit.

"While I'm questioning them one by one, you keep the rest from chatting. And then you can get the boxes that are in the back seat of the car and collect the contents of the bathroom medicine chests and the icebox, being certain that you label each box according to the source of its contents."

"Right," said Brigit.

A big masculine voice boomed above their heads. "It's under the stairs, sir," it said. Tuck stepped back and looked up and saw the medical examiner coming briskly down to the body, black bag firmly in hand. He was followed by a lean fingerprint man who was lighting a cigarette, and a photographer with camera, looking longingly at the view of the hills to the west.

"Hop to it, boys," said Tuck.

"Right," said the medical examiner.

Tuck surveyed the dining-room. He wanted to be able to watch each person as he came in, and yet he did not want to be seated in massive dignity at the foot of the table. He compromised on a chair at one side. The small honey-blonde in the camel's-hair coat came in with her chin high. "She said to tell you my name, so I'm Laurel Byrd," she said.

"Sit here," invited Tuck in his most casual tone, nodding at the big chair at the end of the table. She looked at it dolefully and sat down. He leaned toward her. "The only reason I'm asking each of you a few brief questions alone is that in a mutual discussion each person's memory is blurred and distorted by what the person next to him says. I want a lot of pictures to piece together. No one suspects you of anything."

"Do I look that frightened?" she asked. "I'm not. I screamed, but that was from astonishment."

"You found the body, I hear," said Tuck.

"Yes. Jeff and Woody and I had agreed to meet in the garden before breakfast to decide whether to stay here. I got there first. When I went back to the house to hurry them up, there he was, staring at me."

"What time was this?"

"About eight."

"Then what happened?"

"Everyone burst out of the house; and no one said much, and Tom said 'Cheese' which is not cheese but blasphemy. . . . Am I talking too fast? . . . So then Woody phoned the police and we went up to the tower to wake up André. None of us wanted any breakfast, so we just sat around the living-room not saying anything until the policeman came. Jeff and Woody and I wanted to talk about it, but I think we all had the same idea, that it would look strange to the rest if we went off in a corner and put our heads together."

"Why do you think he was poisoned?"

"Because Denise Morrissey, who is a friend of his, was poisoned. With arsenic. And the doctor who treated her thinks it came from this house. Jeff gave her one of André's sleeping pills, and the doctor came the next day—that was yesterday—to take the box to a chemist for analysis."

Feeling a first, mild tide of interest washing over his brain, he briefed that in his little black book, Laurel Byrd watching him out of clear, young eyes.

"Did Mr. Falkoner have any enemies?"

"I know of two. But it could have nothing to do with this. It was a business matter. And the amount of money involved was only $250 apiece."

"I'd like their names," purred Tuck.

"Larry Harvers and something Nashe. Writers."

"Any more?"

"I don't know. I've been here only a week. I don't know anything about the man. His worst enemy would just have been another person walking in and out to me."

"Let's have a list of the people who've walked in and out since you came here."

She closed her eyes tight and remembered. "Rita Callender. Denise Morrissey. And then there are Ruth and Harold De Lisle—that is, they know him, but they didn't walk in or out."

"Since you've been here."

"Naturally."

"Would you say that these people all liked him?"

"Not all of them. Mrs. Morrissey seems to have. But Rita Callender's in love with him, Harold De Lisle dislikes him moderately, and Ruth De Lisle—dislikes him too, I guess. She suggested strongly that we make tracks away from here, Woody, Jeff and I."

"Do you know the name of the doctor who attended Denise Morrissey?"

"Day. And he lives at The Towers."

"And now," commanded Tuck, "tell me everything that you've seen or heard or thought since the moment you entered this house."

She did.

"I guess that's all," Tuck said at last, and rose politely.

She stood up. "If you want to be *really* reassuring," she said, looking up at him out of clear hazel eyes, "don't have whoever comes in next sit in the chair I did. It was his chair. The feeling is not very comfortable."

He learned nothing new from Jefferson Prince, who, although he seemed still somewhat dazed by what had happened, seemed also to be obscurely enjoying the excitement of it. His blue eyes wre large-pupiled, his thin hands showed just the faintest tremor when 'he lighted a cigarette, one thin lock of his dark hair had escaped the confinement of a gentlemanly amount of hair oil and floated out above his scholar's brow like an inquiring antenna. Tuck learned nothing whatever from him which Laurel Byrd had not already told. When Jeff rose to leave he asked, "It was poison, wasn't it?"

"I think so," Tuck agreed carefully.

Jeff Prince considered the tip of his cigarette and said, "There's irony in that."

André Viaud answered Tuck's questions monosyllabically, and explained that he had left the house the night before shortly after the three young writers had gone, had returned at about midnight to find the house completely dark and apparently empty, and had gone at once to his room. "Usually," he explained, his single elaboration, "I went to the bathroom just off the Red Room to clean my teeth. But I was extremely tired. I didn't go to the Red Room last night."

In the doorway he turned. "I am sorry I couldn't throw more light on the matter of the sleeping capsules. As I said, I find it fantastic to believe that someone was trying to kill me, but I can think of no other reason for arsenic being in those capsules. If it was."

I can, thought Tuck. He watched André Viaud's little checked back disappear toward the living-room, vaguely disturbed by the man's testimony. There was something not quite right about it. Not only his manner, which was almost too deeply unconcerned, but something else. His mind had not succeeded in pinning down what disturbed it when Woody Cornell came swiftly into the room, his brown eyes on Tuck's, his broad, pleasant face devoid of shock or surprise.

Woody Cornell had an objective mind, Tuck found. He talked of murder, and Tuck found his ideas on the subject most unusual for a layman. "I've seen death often enough," he said, "violent and premature death, I mean, to know that it is part of life. Most people react to death as though it were extraordinary. They're wrong, you know. It is only absence of life. What did the old philosopher say? 'When death is, I am not. When I am, death is not. Therefore, why should I be afraid of it?' "

Tuck was even more interested in the two men who had slept on either side of a dead man.

"How was it," he asked the quiet black-haired giant who described himself as Falkoner's secretary, "that you didn't notice the fact that your employer was dead when you went to bed?"

"Tom and I went to the movies," said Jim. "We got home close to one o'clock. Double feature. We were sleepy, I guess, because we usually hit the hay about ten. We undressed in the Red Room and got into our cots in the dark. We thought he was asleep, if we thought anything about it, which we really didn't."

"And this morning when you woke up? It was daylight then."

"Yeah. He still looked just asleep to me. I didn't really look at him. I was thinking more that Mrs. Lovelace wouldn't be back until ten and I had to fix breakfast."

"Mrs. Lovelace is the cook?"

"Yeah. She should of been here by now."

Tom said, "Cheese! Why would I think something was wrong? He was an all-right guy. No one had anything against him."

"After you got into bed last night it was very quiet, wasn't it?"

"Except the crickets," said Tom.

"Didn't you realize that your employer wasn't breathing? Or was he breathing?"

"You couldn't prove it by me," said Tom. "But there's somethin' I do know," he added, his narrow eyes very knowing. "Mr. Falkoner told me about what happened to Mrs. Morrissey. And that box of sleeping pills that Prince gave her one from was up on the mantel where anyone could get at it for a whole day. I saw it there."

"Thank you, Tom," said Tuck.

"O. K.," said Tom.

The medical examiner came into the dining-room as Tom went out. The fingerprint man and the photographer stood in the doorway, watching over their shoulders the two gray-uniformed attendants who were carrying Falkoner's white-swathed body out to the coroner's ambulance.

"It's poison," said the medical examiner, setting his bag on the edge of the table.

"Arsenic?" asked Tuck.

"If it was, the guy was a real stoic. Even if the shock and coma set in unusually early, the gastro-intestinal pain would have made most people run to phone a doctor."

"You can't say definitely that it was arsenic?"

"Not yet. If the stomach contents have anything to say, I'll get the good word to you late tonight or tomorrow. Otherwise, we'll have to find what we can from the organs. That'll take at least a week."

"You want me to take their prints?" asked the fingerprint man, stepping forward as the doctor picked up his black bag. "This has sure been a light day for me so far."

"No," said Tuck. "It won't be necessary."

"I'll send down the pictures tonight," said the photographer. "Didja ever see a better day for outdoor stuff?"

Tuck went to the living-room and found a cadaverous lady in a decent black hat with two red roses saying to Brigit, "I don't know anything about this. I don't know anything at all." Her face was gray and shocked, her eyes frightened.

"Are you Mrs. Lovelace?" asked Tuck.

"Yes. I don't know anything at all."

"Suppose you make us some coffee," suggested Tuck gently. And to Brigit: "Start with the kitchen, Miss Estees. You'd better make a clean sweep of the icebox. Then you can start on the bathrooms. Mrs. Lovelace will, I know, be very helpful."

"I'll do what I can," said Mrs. Lovelace in a limp voice. "But I really don't know anything at all. My brother-in-law just this minute brought me back."

"Do we have to stay here?" asked Laurel Byrd, as soon as Mrs. Lovelace had left.

"Is this your Los Angeles address?" asked Tuck.

"Well, yes. . . ."

"Then you'd better stay here for a while," he suggested.

"Did the medical examiner say it was arsenic?" asked Woody Cornell.

"He doesn't know yet," said Tuck. "Does anyone happen to have the addresses of Harvers, Nashe, Mrs. Morrissey, Dr. Day, Rita Callender, and Harold and Ruth De Lisle?"

"I can get you Mr. Falkoner's address book," offered Jim.

"I'll come along. I want all his private papers."

"There really isn't much," Jim explained as they went down the stairs. "He never kept correspondence. And he just cleaned out his business papers a couple of weeks ago. There's nothing but a few contracts and his bankbook."

"Did he make a will?"

"Not that I know of. His lawyer will know for sure. His name's Goli, and his address is in the book."

Jim unlocked a drawer in the big desk in the corner of the master bedroom with a key which he took from the pocket of the dead man's clothes, neatly hung in the closet. Tuck came up from the Red Room the richer by five contracts, three of them involving Laurel Byrd, Jefferson Prince and Woody Cornell, two of them involving Harvers and Nashe; a red leather address book; and a commercial bankbook of blue imitation leather which told him that Falkoner was worth, in cash, a little over $10,000. He was interested to see that, six months before, he had had on deposit closer to $15,000. He was even more interested to notice that two months before the account had gone up by a deposit of $1,000, and that seven months before it had gone up exactly the same amount, also in a single deposit.

The faces turned toward him expectantly as he entered the living-room.

"If I were you," he said, "I would eat something before too long. You'll have to drive to town, because we're taking everything here with us for analysis. Scudder tells me that you all believe that Mr. Falkoner was poisoned. You are quite right. He was."

The faces still watched him, interested and unafraid.

"So I'd like to know whether there happens to be anything lying around that might have done the trick. Aphis killer? 'Taps for Rats'?"

They all shook their heads from side to side.

"Nothing?" said Tuck.

They shook their heads again.

"Oh, yes, there is," said a voice behind him.

He turned and saw Mrs. Lovelace standing in the doorway, holding a large tray with a shining percolator and half a dozen cups and saucers stiffly level. "There's a pound of roach powder on the third shelf of the middle cupboard in the kitchen. I had to sign my name in some kind of a poison book when I bought it at the drugstore two weeks ago." She added, "They aren't so much roaches as beetles, really. But most unpleasant."

AFTER TUCK and Brigit Estees left, the house seemed very empty. And in a few minutes it seemed even emptier, because Jim and Tom, after a brief conference in one corner of the living-room, went toward the hallway.

"We're going to get something to eat," Jim said. "The icebox is empty. We'll bring back some food. Mr. Falkoner always gave me enough money the first of the month to take care of that."

When she heard the sound of a car leaving, Laurel suddenly wondered whether Jim and Tom had taken the gray Buick coupé, which they had always used before, or the black car. She went swiftly to the door and opened it and saw the gray Buick vanishing down the earth road, followed by a wake of dust. She walked across the bridge to the three-car garage which flanked the road to the left of the house. The low gleaming car in the dim, oil-smelling cavern expressed for her, for a moment, the fallacy of belief in possession.

He may have the pink slip to prove his ownership of this car in some drawer or some wallet, she thought. *But he never really owned it at all. He rented it, for a little while.* She laid one small hand on the rear fender, and the feel of the smooth cold metal brought home to her for the first time the solid and frightening fact of Falkoner's death.

As she opened the front door of the house she heard a dismal, whooshing sound from the living-room. Jeff, Woody, and André, wearing trapped expressions, were watching Mrs. Lovelace as she vacuumed the turquoise rug. Jeff's feet were drawn into the air to let her attack the space before his chair. Mrs. Lovelace had no expression at all on her haggard face. On her head was a white mobcap with a cotton-lace ruffle.

"Do you really have to clean just now?" Laurel asked Mrs. Lovelace's ear.

"I always clean on Fridays," Mrs. Lovelace stated, and made for Woody's chair. He rose hurriedly.

"Let's get out of here," he said.

They went to Don the Beachcomber's again, out of an overwhelming inertia, coupled with physical discomfort. When Jeff said, "The Beachcomber's O. K.?" everyone nodded mechanically. They were packed so tightly in the car that even a nod was an achievement.

"Whisky would be good," said Woody.

The first person they saw on entering the narrow room with its bamboo bar, its bamboo chairs, was Rita Callender. She was talking earnestly at a fair young man in a gray sport coat who nodded continuously. Her hair was piled high on her head; she was wearing a beige coat with beige fox fur; her chin was in one hand, a cigarette in the other. She beckoned them with the cigarette. "How is the gentleman *aux* carrots?" she asked Laurel.

Woody looked around the crowded place, and then drew out a chair for Laurel. She sat down facing Rita. Jeff sat beside her, Woody at one end of the table, André at the other. Woody caught a waiter's eye; motivated, Laurel was sure, by a desire to fortify himself against Rita Callender's reaction to the news of Falkoner's death.

Laurel introduced Jeff and Woody to Rita. Rita introduced the young man beside her, a perennial juvenile in his late twenties.

"What will you have, Laurel?" Jeff asked, sharing the cocktail list with her. "I'm going to settle for a

Scotch and soda."

"So will I," said Laurel, wondering if any drink in the world would make her feel normal again.

"I'll have a Daiquiri," said André.

"Three Scotch and sodas," said Woody to the waiter. "And a Daiquiri."

Rita was saying to the young man beside her, "Peter, these four people live with the most amazing man I've ever met. The 'Grow-Young-with-Buttermilk' type. Absolutely a character." She looked at Laurel and said, "Don't let him smell whisky on your breath, my dear. He has a lecture all about an actress he once knew who took to drink and now sells flowers in front of Grauman's Chinese."

"Alcohol never did anything to anyone that a good sanitarium couldn't cure," said the perennial juvenile.

"And you know, don't you, darling?" said Rita. Her murky eyes sought their faces. "Isn't he marvelous?" But her voice told Laurel that Rita knew he wasn't.

"Drinking to excess," said André surprisingly and gravely, "is a symptom. The cures don't cure anything, because the basic maladjustment that makes the person drink is still there."

"André," said Rita to Peter, "has been drunk once in his life, the sweet thing."

"Once," said André, "was enough."

The waiter set the tall glass down in front of Laurel, and suddenly the moment went strange and crazy. It seemed absurd to her that the death of the man who hated alcohol should have stranded them here in this preposterous place, talking with a shallow and perhaps psychopathic woman who would in the next few minutes have to learn about this man's death from their lips.

"What do you think about what happened to Mrs. Morrissey?" Jeff asked Rita, skirting Falkoner's death.

Rita looked genuinely interested for the first time. "I really don't get it. I mean, what goes on? She doesn't seem to have the slightest notion how it happened."

"None of us does," said André. "Do you?"

"Not the vaguest," said Rita. "I mean, no one could possibly have wanted to do the gal in, and she certainly didn't get full of world-weariness and decide on a quick exit. She and the world get along fine. So that pretty much makes the thing an accident, doesn't it?"

"Arsenic by accident," Woody murmured. "No."

"No, not after what happened to Falkoner," Jeff said. All of a sudden it was very still and Laurel heard a woman's voice from a near-by table say, "—had a perfectly rotten break, because then they cut the scene."

She couldn't take her eyes from Rita, although she felt almost indecent looking at her. Nothing much changed about her face. She continued looking at Jeff, and said in a scarcely altered voice, "What's happened to him?"

"He's dead," said Woody. "He's been poisoned." He was looking at Rita too, with a curiosity which was not at all unkind.

Rita looked from Jeff to him, and still her face did not change. One hand went out volitionlessly to the ash tray; her cigarette dropped into it; she withdrew her hand and stared at the red end of the cigarette, glowing among the gray ashes, the burned-out stubs in the tray. She stood up in one long motion and moved swiftly down the room to a door at its far end.

They finished their drinks and ordered lunch. Still Rita had not returned. Peter, who had taken Rita's disappearance equably enough, began to grow a little agitated, an agitation which he showed by lighting cigarettes, taking a puff and putting them out immediately.

Finally he turned squarely to Laurel. "I wonder. Would you mind very much? You see, we have to meet some people in half an hour."

"Would I mind what?" asked Laurel.

"Getting her. I can't, you know."

"No, I wouldn't mind," said Laurel, minding very much.

She opened the door onto the small powder room with its bamboo chair, its long mirror opposite the door. Rita was standing in front of the mirror. She was looking at her own grimace of agony in the glass.

Seeing Laurel's reflection beside her own, she put both hands over her face. "It hurts. It hurts," she whispered harshly. "For God's sake, go away."

When Laurel was sipping her coffee, Rita came back. Only the whites of her eyes showed that she had been weeping—they were slightly bloodshot. Impassively, she said, scarcely moving her painted lips, "Take me home, Pete."

Pete stood up. He was benign and very reasonable. "Oh, come on now, darling. Why go home and brood among the family portraits? What you need is a drink."

He turned to beckon the waiter. Rita stood immovable beside the bamboo chair. Soothing Hawaiian music was about her. Nothing of Rita moved but her knees. She sat down smoothly and effortlessly, and groped for the package of cigarettes at Peter's place. "Perhaps you're right," she said.

"ROACH powder," said Tuck, as he and Brigit drove down the twisted road that led to Hollywood proper, the contents of the boxes in the back seat rattling furiously, "has two distinct advantages. It is tasteless and odorless. Quite recently it was mistaken for powdered eggs by the cook at a large private insane asylum, with the result that a lot of euthanasia happened. Second, it is frequently pure sodium fluoride. A teaspoonful will kill. It can be bought at the nearest druggist by the pound package."

"And thirdly," said Brigit, "in this case there happened to be a pound of it on the third shelf of the middle cupboard, in plain sight."

"You," said Tuck, "are five feet eleven inches tall in your stocking feet. I am six feet five. Whether it would have been in the plain sight of Laurel Byrd, Woody Cornell or André Viaud, I doubt. Furthermore, you have already decided that Falkoner was killed with it, and that's bad. We're a long way from diddling with theories yet. We've got leg work to do."

"There's nothing wrong with my legs," said Brigit.

"But are they good for walking with?"

"That's what they do best," said Brigit cheerfully.

Tuck reached into his trousers pocket and pulled out a handful of silver. "Got a nickel?"

"Sure." She dived into her large, sparsely packed purse. "What for?"

"As soon as we hit town, I'm going to phone Gufferty for legal permission to make a few inquiries at Falkoner's bank. I'm interested in two large deposits.

If they were made by check, which is most probable, I can find out who made them."

"Blackmail!" pounced Brigit.

"Maybe. Money, alcohol and love are the three hot bets for general motives when someone turns up dead, and the greatest of these is money."

"What do we do after we prowl among the debits and credits?"

"We'll go have a look at the people who walked in and out."

Brigit snapped her fingers. "I didn't tell you. When I went in the kitchen to raid the icebox, I saw a milk bottle, rinsed out and turned upside down on the sink. There was a milk-bottle cap in the sink strainer. It said 'Buttermilk.' Mrs. Lovelace was making the coffee then, so I asked her about it. She told me that Mr. Falkoner always drank buttermilk—he didn't want to gain weight. Furthermore, he always drank a glass at night before he went to bed. Furthermore, no one else in the place touched it except Falkoner. Furthermore, everyone in the place knew that he did, and that everyone else didn't."

"Poisoned buttermilk is about the worst way to die that I can think of, offhand," said Tuck.

The manager was discussing an FHA loan with a man and this wife. He looked at the writ and Tuck's shield and said, "The chief clerk's the person you want." He rose to a tiptoe position and craned his neck in order to look over the dark wooden partition which separated the front office from the space behind the tellers' windows. "Mr. Slimm!" he called.

A brisk young man in a clean white shirt and a bright blue sport coat hustled into the front office. He had blazing blue eyes and a sassy, pleasant smile. The manager explained who Tuck was and what he wanted.

"Come right along with me," beckoned Mr. Slimm. "We'll find what you want in a jiffy."

Tuck and Brigit passed into the sanctum behind the tellers' windows, where three adding machines were clattering maddeningly, manned by three men in shirt sleeves whose agile fingers pattered with unbelievable speed up the array of round black keys.

"You know anything about banking?" asked Mr. Slimm.

"Nothing," said Tuck.

"It's life," said Mr. Slimm simply. "I raise my hand." He raised it. "That consumed a certain amount of energy. To replace it, I'm going to have to eat a certain amount of food. Debit and credit. Everything balances in life. Everything balances in a bank. What do you want to know?"

Tuck handed him the little blue book and looked down over Mr. Slimm's shoulder to point out the two identical deposits of $1,000. "I want to know where that money came from."

Mr. Slimm leafed through the small inky pages. He looked up brightly. "Here's a story. Up to eight months ago, deposits total more than withdrawals. After that, the opposite. He lost his job."

He beckoned a teller who had just closed his window and they went together back to the great vault, which Mr. Slimm unlocked, and which they both entered. In a few moments they emerged, and Mr. Slimm swung the imposing door shut, locking it with a most unimposing key. He went to the bare length of black linoleum at the end of the long counter where the tellers stood, and set down two long narrow boxes.

"In here," he said, pointing to one, "are all the commercial deposit slips for July of last year. The first deposit you're interested in was made on July 10." His swift fingers moved along the packets of papers which the box contained, and drew out a sheaf of deposit slips, stapled together at the top. "Here are the deposit slips received across·the counter on July 10." He riffled through the booklet, and then paused, and holding it open with one hand while he pointed with the forefinger of the other, he extended the book toward Tuck. Tuck saw a pale green slip, with Falkoner's name and address at the top, and a deposit of $1,000 inked boldly on the first line. Mr. Slimm's forefinger pointed to the number beside it. "The deposit was in the form of a check. That number stands for the bank on which the check was drawn. It happens to be another branch of this same bank. It's the Hollywood and Vine branch. That's where you'll go to find out who signed the check that credited Mr. Falkoner's account with $1,000, because that account will be debited by the same amount, on either July 11 or July 12. It takes a day for a check to get through the clearing house."

"But what if more than one account is debited for that amount on July 11 or July 12?" asked Brigit.

"That's *very* unlikely," said Mr. Slimm. But her question seemed to cause him chagrin. In a moment he brightened. "Now for the second deposit, made on—" he opened the bankbook and glanced at it—"November 1, last year." He almost skipped over to the second of the long boxes, and again withdrew a stapled packet of deposit slips, which he riffled through absorbedly. He came back to them with a fallen face. "Cash," he said. "No way of tracing cash."

He hurried to a filing cabinet and slid open one of the green metal drawers. He beckoned them. "This is what you're looking fot." He withdrew a square of heavy yellow paper, pointed to a column marked *Debits*. "Somewhere in this column, an item of $1,000. And see?" He pointed to the head of the page, where, neatly typed in capital letters, Tuck read the name *Irma P.*

Buckley, with an address just below it. "That name," said Mr. Slimm, "will be the name of the person you want."

"Unless we find more than one debit of $1,000," said Brigit, doggedly.

"That's very, *very* unlikely," said Mr. Slimm. Again he looked momentarily chagrined at this lack of perfection. But again he brightened almost at once. He also looked conspiratorial. "Say," he asked, "what do you want this bird for?"

"Maybe murder," said Tuck.

"Debit!" said Mr. Slimm.

Mr. Slimm had prophesied correctly. At ten minutes to three Brigit yelled, "I've got it!"

Tuck went quickly to her side, and read: *Mrs. Ruth De Lisle, 1200 Da Vente Road, Bel-Air, California.*

"I don't believe it!" said Ruth De Lisle, when Tuck told her that Falkoner was dead of poison. "I quite simply don't believe it."

"Why not?" asked Tuck, quietly.

"He wasn't *important* enough. He wasn't important enough for anyone to kill."

"And I suppose suicide is out?" asked Tuck.

"Oh, *yes!*" said Ruth De Lisle. "I mean, I should think so. Earl Falkoner was such an egotist, you know." She suddenly leaned back against the dull green sofa. "This is a shock," she said in her clear lovely voice, which did not sound at all shocked.

"I've just been going through his bankbook," said Tuck. "On July 10 he deposited a check from you for $1,000."

Ruth De Lisle's head turned toward him slowly and gracefully. "Yes. That's quite true."

"I'm curious about that check," Tuck confessed.

"Naturally. It was a business matter."

"I assumed of course that it was. What sort of business?"

"I'll tell you the whole story. After he left the studio, a month or so after, he came over to see me, as he occasionally did. He had a wonderful idea for a screen original, he said, which was so good he had already sold it simply on the story alone, but he could make more money on the deal if he hired a couple of writers to put it down in detail. He didn't, it seems, feel that he could afford the thousand or so it would take to pay the salaries of the writers. Other irons in the fire, et cetera."

She curled one leg under her, and settled herself comfortably. "You never heard him talk, of course. He was good at it. He fixed his eyes on you—I have always felt that he had done some reading up on hypnotism—and the words burbled out in torrents, with gestures. I don't know how he did it, but before long I was full of the conviction that his idea was the *best* idea since *The Birth of a Nation*. I wrote a check for the money he wanted, in exchange for a quarter interest in the show. An oral quarter interest. As soon as he had gone I began to regret what I'd done. I even thought of stopping payment on the check, but you don't do things like that to people you know, and anyway I had guests coming for dinner."

Her face hardened just a trifle. "Time went by. Some months later I happened to find myself sitting with him at a party. No one else was with us, so I mentioned the story—how it was coming, when it would be sold, and so forth. He was very straightforward. Two good men were hard at work on it. . . . It was going to take a little longer than he had first supposed—and then some people came over and the subject was dropped.

"Some more time went by. And then Harold and I were shopping and I saw a fur jacket I wanted badly. Harold said to get it, but I said I'd spent too much on

clothes lately, and he looked all at once suspicious. I
realized that I'd used a sizable sum of money very
foolishly. I also realized that I'd not told him about
it. And that now I couldn't tell him about it. You see,
there was an oil well two years ago. . . . I invested without telling Harold, who is ever so smart about such
things. That oil well was a gold brick, Mr. Tuck.
Harold was really very sweet, in an impatient sort of
way. He made me promise that I'd *never* put any
money into anything without telling him. He said I
was *very* susceptible."

"So you don't want me to say anything about the
thousand dollars to your husband, is that it?" asked
Tuck.

"You mustn't!" said Ruth De Lisle solemnly.

"I'll do the best I can," said Tuck. "Why didn't
you discuss Falkoner's proposition with your husband?"

"I *told* you. He wasn't there when Earl was making
his little speech, and I wrote the check under the influence. And then there were the people in for dinner,
and I couldn't tell Harold then, and time just went by,
that's all. And then, when I knew or was fairly sure
I'd been had, it was too late. I was really afraid to."

"When did you know you'd been had?" asked Tuck.

"Well, one morning I woke up with the thing prey-
ing on my mind. Harold went riding—I've never learned
to like horses—so I phoned Earl and told him to come
up, that I wanted to talk with him. And that was a
terrible half-hour, Mr. Tuck. I think Earl had guessed
from the tone of my voice on the phone what I wanted
to say. He came in very brisk and assured, full of good
reports about the story. When I brought up the fact
that I expected some return—and soon—on my invest-
ment, he asked me carelessly if I'd told Harold about
it. I said I hadn't. And then, all at once, he was looking at me with that smile of his. 'A funny thing has

occurred to me, Ruth,' he said. 'It's too bad you didn't tell Harold. I mean, in this town, it looks so sort of funny for a woman to write a man a check for $1,000.' Oh, he was very oblique. He changed the subject at once. But I knew I'd been had."

"A skunk," briefed Tuck.

Her prominent green eyes clouded with thoughts. "To you and me, yes." She looked at Tuck. "But does a skunk smell bad to himself? What I mean is: I don't think for a moment that Earl saw himself as a swindler. I think he rationalized what he'd done so that it looked all right from where he sat. So few real-life villains, I think, are like Richard the Third. They don't know they're villains. The inner decay is so gradual that they never notice it."

She became reflective. "In a way, I'm a little sorry for Earl. He'd come a long way from Texas, on a great deal of bluff and a certain talent for imagining big and gorgeous sets. I think that when he died, he was on his way back to Texas. I think that on gray mornings, or when he was waiting for sleep to come, he knew it. The trick he played on me was a last and desperate stand. Success to him meant money. Therefore he needed money. The play was just an elaborate device his subconscious had worked out to prove to himself that he wasn't a cheat."

Tuck felt rather cruel as he let loose the punch to the solar plexus he had been withholding.

"I can understand all you've said. You've convinced me. But why did you fall for the trick a second time? How did he manage to mesmerize that second thousand dollars—in cash—out of you?"

"But I never gave him a second thousand dollars," said Ruth De Lisle, wide-eyed.

Tuck stared at her. She stared back. Tuck looked down at his clasped hands, across which he had been leaning. "I see," he said.

He looked up at Ruth De Lisle. "Do you know anyone," he said, "who could conceivably have poisoned both Denise Morrissey and Earl Falkoner?"

Ruth De Lisle adjusted her mind to the sudden change of subject. "No," she said, after a short pause. "No one."

"My wife is so veddy sporting," said a voice from the doorway, and Tuck turned his head to see a small square man in riding clothes striding into the room. Tuck wondered how long he had stood just around the edge of the door, listening.

"Did you have a nice ride, dear?" asked Ruth De Lisle, extending a hand which her husband held briefly and let fall.

"So-so."

"This is Miss Estees—and Mr. Tuck. My husband." She looked up at him. "It seems that Earl's dead, dear. Mr. Tuck's investigating."

"I gathered that from the remark I caught as I came in," said Mr. De Lisle. "Too bad. When did it happen?"

"He was found dead in bed this morning. The time of death has not been accurately established," Tuck informed him. "What did you mean when you said your wife was so very sporting?"

Harold De Lisle flicked his gleaming tan boot with his crop. "Silly of me, I am sure. Doesn't mean anything, I'm certain. But I couldn't help remembering a night we all sat up late talking about murder. I couldn't help remembering what Rita Callender said that night."

"Which was?" probed Tuck.

"I don't like the Callender," said Harold De Lisle. "You should know that; I think, from the start. It was like this. I had just made the statement regarding murder that there was only one circumstance, which in my opinion justified it. Blackmail." He looked casually at his wife out of tiny eyes which were as hard as black glass. "I discoursed a bit, I'm afraid, and said that the only one of the basic drives which makes a man different from the lower animals is the one called by most psychologists 'the desire to render aid.' A blackmailer, who trades on other people's weaknesses, proves himself to lack that drive, and therefore cannot be classified as a fully developed human being. Since he does not classify as a human being, the rules regarding one's treatment of human beings, the chief of which is 'Thou shalt not kill,' do not hold good with regard to one's treatment of a blackmailer. I was simply playing with words. The wine was in, the wit was posturing rather absurdly. But when I finished speaking, there was a silence. I remember thinking that, to the susceptible, my reasoning might have carried a bit of conviction."

"Where does Callender come into the picture?" asked Tuck.

"Oh, yes. She had been sitting on that large ottoman over there—" he pointed with his riding crop— "trying to look very interesting. She is one of those annoying people who have trained themselves to top everything you say. 'I can think of a better reason for murder,' I remember her saying, in that whisky tenor of hers. She waited until everyone was looking at her, pretending to be quite unconscious of the fact that they were looking, brooding down at the embers in the fireplace. 'Hate is a better reason,' she said. 'Pure, simple, unsubtle hate, like the hatred of Cain for Abel.' Rita hates Denise Morrissey, Mr. Tuck."

"Why?"

"Because Falkoner always treated Denise with a certain respect. Partly, of course, because when they first met, Denise had been the boss's wife. But partly because Denise is a lady. He treated Rita, on the other hand, with something very much like contempt. Rita is not a lady. She drinks too much. Falkoner, you see, was one of those simple men, for whom there can be only two kinds of women—ladies and tarts.

"I'm not sure," added Harold De Lisle, "that he wasn't right, you know."

"And now," said Tuck, getting out his little black notebook and his stubby pencil, "where were the two of you last night from six on?"

Harold De Lisle's black eyes sparkled with anger. His wife saw the look and interpreted it. She went quickly to his side and put a hand on his arm. "It's just a formality, dear." She faced Tuck. "Harold was at home all evening. I left at about seven and returned at about eight-thirty, and spent the rest of the evening in. Some friends dropped by."

"Where did you go when you left at about seven?"

"Down to the Boulevard. Everything's open Thursday night, you know. I had forgotten to buy a wedding present for a little friend of mine who's getting married tomorrow. I was reminded of it when Denise told me she was toying with the idea of marrying Earl Falkoner."

"Oh," said Tuck, "he'd asked her to marry him."

"Not yet," said Ruth De Lisle. "But then, that's always the last thing, isn't it? I mean, any woman usually can tell when a man's mind is sidling around the idea. She'd had several indications. She's been rather lonely, of course, since Joel died."

"And what did you say about it?" Tuck asked, looking hard at Ruth De Lisle.

She spread her hands artlessly. "What could I say? I learned years ago that there's absolutely *no use* in telling a woman who wants to marry a man that the man's no good. She simply dislikes you for it. And I'm really rather fond of Denise."

Harold De Lisle's eyes were sparkling again, this time with amusement. "Women," he said to the ceiling, "are wonderful."

CHAPTER NINE
SPEAKING OF POISONS

RITA CALLENDER lived in St. James Place, the most exclusive street in Los Angeles, exclusive in the literal sense of the word, for it is just two blocks long, with wrought-iron gates at each end. Tuck parked the black car near the sign saying, *All Deliveries Must Be Made via the Alley*, and he and Brigit passed through the portals. The deliberately splendid, haughtily ugly old houses faced each other across the sunny street like *grandes dames* at a dinner table.

"I haven't seen lace curtains since I was a little girl," marveled Brigit.

"Keep your eye peeled for a pair of spanking bays," advised Tuck.

The house where Rita lived was colonial and red brick. The white door was opened by Rita's mother, a stumpy woman with mournful eyes. She told them that Rita had risen at twelve and departed with a young man for lunch. The death of Falkoner did not move her one way or another. "She will go around with odd people," said Mrs. Callender. "I don't know why. She has really everything. But she will do it. I'll tell her you called."

Larry Harvers also lived in Los Angeles, on a vigorously middle-class street where every other house was a stucco box containing four flats. The houses that weren't flats were tan and clapboard with deep eaves and small lawns, or else brown-shingle, two-story places that did not seem to belong at all to the squat palm trees on each half of the front lawn which was inevitably bisected by a cement walk leading uncompromisingly to the front door. Larry Harvers, they found, lived in a trailer parked beside the driveway at the rear of one of these. He peered at them through a small square window which just held his face, and opened the door.

"I'm Lieutenant Tuck, of the Los Angeles Homicide Squad," Tuck said. "I have to ask you a few questions."

"Come in," invited Harvers. They did, and Tuck felt the walls pressing in on his brain. The little room would be well peopled with Harvers alone inside. With Tuck and Brigit there too, it gave him the distinct feeling of burial alive.

When Tuck told him of Falkoner's death, Harvers's little eyes went round with surprise. "No! Really!" He leaned forward almost avidly. "How did he die?"

"Poison."

Harvers thought for a minute. "Say. Maybe you can tell me. Aren't I right in believing that you can sue the estate of a dead man?"

Tuck was mildly startled. "Yes. You're right."

"Whee!" said Harvers, bringing his plump hands together in a soundless clap. "We collect." He looked straight at Tuck. "He owes a friend and me $500."

"I know. There's something else I want to know. What did you do last night?"

"I didn't move a muscle. I lay right there on that bunk on which you're sitting rather uncomfortably, I fear, and finished reading *The Dove's Nest.* Have you read it?" They shook their heads, and he said earnestly in a voice full of interest and respect, "Katherine Mansfield's one of the great modern writers, I think. It's a pity she died so young." And his big face really looked decently grave as he spoke. "Slender," he said. "Very slender, and sometimes slim. But *fine.*" He saw their faces and his own changed. "I suppose you want to

question Nashe too. You can't until Monday unless you
feel like a trip. to Laguna. He's spending the week-end
with some friends there. Dead, huh? And poison."
He looked reflective. "You know, it's somehow right
that it should have been poison. I can't explain what
I mean, but it's somehow *right*. Perhaps it's the delicate
undertone of irony to it. Raw vegetables, wheaten bread,
buttermilk, and poison at the last."

Dr. Day's wife told Tuck that he would be home in
an hour and a half. Tuck emerged from the telephone
booth and said to Brigit, "If I eat something, I'll get
very sleepy. If I don't eat something, I'll stop caring
whether we talk to Dr. Day and Denise Morrissey and
maybe Rita Callender before we call it a day. It's a
hard choice."

"There's always coffee," said Brigit callously.

Tuck felt himself brighten. "There is," he agreed.

He wedged himself onto an impossibly .small stool
before the long counter, where a row of early diners
were reading papers while they ate, or chewing doggedly,
their eyes still full of the day's worries.

They ordered the special dinner. Tuck looked at
their two faces reflected back at him from the mirror
along the wall in back of the counter. He saw a woman's
round face framed by dazzling orange hair, a face which
even the unkind glare of the fluorescent lights above could
not rob of a certain bland wholesomeness. And next
to hers he saw his own face, long, sallowly tan, with
narrow brown eyes and deep lines bracketing the mouth.
"Why do they always have mirrors behind the counters
of drugstores?" he asked. "It takes away your appetite."

A small bowl of thin vegetable soup appeared on the
buff linoleum counter before him. He salted it. "When
I was a kid, a drugstore was really a nice place." He
tapped the counter. "None of this linoleum. Marble.

And the smell of drugs. No rubber bathing caps. No syringes. No sunglasses. And one man did everything, and he was usually a gossip, so that the drugstore was the clearinghouse for local scandal. And while you had your cherry phosphate, you learned that Mr. Wilkins had left his wife. And there was a lot of time to wonder why."

"I have a theory," said Brigit.

"I was afraid you might," said Tuck. "All right. Let's have it."

"Everyone in the house could have known about the roach powder. But that's not all. Visitors to the house could have known about it too. It was in the same closet as the glasses. So anyone who went to the kitchen for a glass of water in the last two weeks could have seen it. And could have known it was poison by having read about the insane-asylum poisonings you were telling me about when we left Falkoner's today."

"Granted," said Tuck.

"What we don't know is who had the desire to kill Falkoner. Poison strikes me this way: it argues premeditation. A fit of murderous rage would express itself in a more violent method. So the desire to kill Falkoner must have existed before the murderer saw the roach powder. I mean, it's ridiculous to suppose that the means of killing the man and the arousal of the impulse to kill him were simultaneous."

"Those coincidences *will* happen, though," commented Tuck. " 'The time, the place and the hated one all together.' "

Ignoring his liberty with Browning, Brigit went on: "I believe we can eliminate three people to start with. The writers who didn't know Falkoner was alive until a week ago. We eliminate also the two other writers, because Laurel Byrd told you that although they visited the house the day before the guy died, they did not leave the living-room. For the same reason, the Morrissey woman washes out. So who's left? The cook, the two muscle men, and Rita Callender. Rita, remember, was alone in the living-room when Laurel Byrd came upstairs. She could have gone to the kitchen, seen the poison and done the dirty."

"The motive being, I suppose, 'Hell hath no fury like a woman scorned.'"

"Well," Brigit demanded, "what's the matter with that?"

"Nothing, because it hasn't."

"How do you like my theory?" asked Brigit.

"It's wonderful," said Tuck. "It's logical. It has simplicity. But it depends on the fact that Falkoner was poisoned with sodium fluoride, and that fact hasn't been established yet. It's always rather dangerous to formulate theories without facts to draw from. It's a little like building a house with the notion of slipping the foundation under it later."

"Don't be smug," said Brigit. "I admit that we're just playing. Don't you think it's more fun than talking about the evolution of the drugstore?"

"And there's something else wrong with your theory," said Tuck. "Something badly wrong. It ignores the fact that Denise Morrissey nearly died of arsenic poisoning."

"Yes," admitted Brigit emptily. "It does, doesn't it?"

Tuck grinned at her. "And it's relying a little too heavily on the power of coincidence, much as I respect chance, to assume that Denise Morrissey just happened to ingest a fatal dose of arsenic the day before Falkoner died of it. In fact, if there's one thing I'm sure of, it's that there's an intimate association between those two happenings." He watched his hot beef sandwich approach in the hands of a thin and agile young man behind the counter, and wished that he had ordered something else.

"Aw, come on," said Brigit. "You're among friends."

"I have several theories. They're all as bad as yours. Because they depend on the fact that there was poison in that box of capsules, and we don't know yet whether or not that's true. But supposing that there was—why, then the poisoning of Denise is explained. It was pure accident. A very young man, taken by her, wanting to direct her attention to him by doing something for her, learned that she had been suffering from sleeplessness, went up to André Viaud's tower room to get her some phenobarbital, not knowing, of course, that arsenic had been substituted, and that the white capsules in the box each contained a dose of death. And I rather like that part of it. It has the craziness of life in it. Denise took one before retiring, and called a doctor in time.

"There are only two possible explanations of why arsenic had been substituted for the phenobarbital. André Viaud had planned to kill someone. Someone was trying to kill André Viaud.

"And now we get very supposititious indeed. First, let's assume that André Viaud was trying to kill someone by giving him one of those capsules of arsenic, and furthermore that the someone was Falkoner. In that case, he would have been incredibly foolhardy to go doggedly ahead with his plans after learning that Denise had nearly died and that the doctor who attended her included André's poison box among the possible sources of the poison. So he must have poisoned Falkoner before learning about Denise. Which would mean that Falkoner was already dead when he was ordering those flowers for Mrs. Morrissey. It would also mean that André Viaud felt a trap close about him when the doctor came for the capsules, and was helpless. And that is borne out by the one single fact. When I questioned him in the dining-room, he was monosyllabic, careful, nerveless. He made me think of a man who has already visioned the bitter end and has resigned himself to the mercy of circumstances. I thought also that he rather stressed his complete puzzlement about the possibility that there may have been poison in his box of sleeping capsules. But there I may be wrong, because I am the first to admit that such a discovery would be very puzzling.

"The second supposition is that someone was trying to kill André Viaud. His plan went awry when Mrs. Morrissey got the poison instead, and Dr. Day came and took the box away. The rest of this theory is somewhat like the first. That someone wanted to kill Falkoner also, and had poisoned him before Dr. Day came."

He looked at the clock. "There's just a chance," he said, "that the medical examiner will be able to tell us which theory is nearer the truth."

"I'll phone him," said Brigit eagerly. "The sight of you in a phone booth gives me claustrophobia."

"Fine," said Tuck. "But I want to talk with him too. I don't know too much about the way arsenic works."

"You're pretty sure of yourself, aren't you?" asked Brigit, fumbling in her change purse.

Tuck pushed a nickel toward her.

Brigit came out of the booth. "Arsenic," she said. "He's holding the line."

Tuck learned quite a bit about arsenic. He learned that it occurs in two forms, pentavalent and trivalent. He learned that the body had to reduce the pentavalent form to the trivalent form before it could suffer and die. He learned that the medical examiner could not give him a pat answer as to when the poison was taken, because it depended upon whether the powder had been fine or coarse, which he did not know; whether it had been in organic combination with another substance, which he did not know; whether Falkoner had any tolerance to the poison, which he did not know. He did commit himself on three points. First, that Falkoner had died not before eleven and not later than one o'clock; second, that the terminal anoxia occurred anywhere from an hour to twenty-four hours after the ingestion of the poison; and third, that Falkoner had been extraordinarily stoic, if he called no doctor at the onset of the symptoms.

"What now?" asked Brigit, who had been standing with her nose pressed against the glass of the booth.

"Now you begin to look for our poisoner. You do it in this way. You go to every drugstore in Hollywood —try Hollywood first, and if you have no luck, work away from it into Los Angeles—and ask to examine the poison register. Go back at least two weeks for a start. Make a list of every name. Ask the druggist for descriptions. He won't remember a thing about anyone, so thank him nicely, and try another store. . . . Stop from time to time to eat," he added. "And you can take the car."

The Towers was on the Sunset Strip. It was owned, Tuck happened to know, by an extremely voluptuous screen star with a good head on her shoulders. It looked like money and dancing at the Trocadero and clear celluloid florist's boxes, and vaguely like ladies of virtue not easy but most expensive. It was the tallest building in Hollywood, built just before an earthquake which left an aftermath of cracked plaster and height restrictions.

Denise Morrissey had been crying. She was wearing a house-coat of ice-blue satin; he noticed two dull pear-shaped spots on the bosom where her tears had fallen. Her eyes were faintly red-dimmed, as blondes' eyes always are when they cry; there were violet circles beneath them which were rather becoming because they carried, with Denise's slender pallor, just the faintest suggestion of the lady with the camellias.

"I'm Lieutenant Tuck, of the—."

· "I know," said Denise Morrissey, in a dull voice. "Rita Callender phoned a little while ago. Come in, please."

The first thing Tuck saw was a great mound of gardenias in a crystal bowl. Their dull rich white petals were faintly creamy with the first trace of their inevitable decay, and the room was full of their odor.

After waving him to a rose satin chair, she sat very straight on the end of a blue brocade sofa, the billow of gold taffeta eiderdown at its other end bearing mute witness to the fact that she had been lying down when he rang. "Please," she said, "please be just as brief as possible."

"I will. Tell me what you did last night."

Her blue eyes opened a trifle. "I was right here. All evening. Didn't you know about the poisoning? I had to have a nurse all day. It was terrible."

"You say all day. When exactly did she leave?"

"After she fixed me some soup at about six. I had to be on a liquid diet, you know. The soup was the first real food I'd had, except for the champagne."

"The champagne?"

"Yes. You see, I can't stand milk. Ice cream is what I especially hate, but I can't stand milk either. So I told her I couldn't drink milk and she suggested champagne. Earl was really rather alarmed about me, I think."

"Earl Falkoner?"

She nodded. "Yes. He came in about eight." Her eyes began to mist over.

"Was he in good spirits?"

"Oh, yes." The mild and depthless blue eyes were looking straight into his. Then the look faltered to the handkerchief wadded in her hand. "Oh, God," she whispered, "I can't believe it!" She looked up at him.

"That's the way these terrible things always are. It takes such a long time before they become true." The handkerchief was suddenly pressing against her mouth. Her eyes evaded his, and she drew in a stifled sigh through the fine white linen. The sigh came out in tears which ran abruptly out of the pink corners of her eyes and down her white cheeks.

"You were very fond of him, weren't you?"

She nodded her head, but did not speak. The handkerchief was pressed hard against her lips for a long minute, and then the hand holding it dropped lifelessly into her satin lap. "Very," she said.

"Do you have any idea, Mrs. Morrissey, any idea at all, how you happened to be poisoned day before yesterday?"

She shrugged limply. Even those few tears had been a spending of more energy than she had. "None at all. For a while I thought it might have been that capsule the nice young man at Earl's got for me, but Dr. Day stopped past a little while before you came to see how I was, and it seems there was no arsenic in the box. Only phenobarbital."

"I beg your pardon?" said Tuck, feeling a tepid shock run all over his body.

"Phenobarbital," she repeated. She reached suddenly forward and touched one of the yellowing flowers on the Chippendale coffee table before the sofa. The diamond on the slender hand blazed briefly with the swift motion.

THE poor and beautiful secretary paced her simple little room, which was 30 by 40 feet, wearing simple white satin lounging pajamas, wondering whether she should marry her boss, who was rich and handsome but not so good, or the young saxophonist who was good and handsome, but not so rich.

It could end only one of two ways, Laurel decided. The woman she saw her boss kissing would turn out to be his sister, and the musician would brain someone with his saxophone, and she'd marry the boss. Or the woman she saw her boss kissing wouldn't be his sister, and the secretary would run away from his apartment leaving the champagne to get warm on the table, straight into the arms of the young saxophonist, and they'd all go home sorry to see Ginger Rogers lose a cool million, but glad to learn that there were a few nice girls left.

She glanced over at Jeff. He was watching the shadows on the screen, smiling. Woody was as intent on the story as a child. André's eyes were closed.

Shocked, she remembered that the four of them had seen a man lying dead that morning.

Although none of them admitted it, their exuberant acceptance of her proposal that they eat dinner in town, Laurel knew, was due to a disinclination to return to the house on the hill any sooner than necessary. "We should phone Mrs. Lovelace, though," she said.

"Yes," said Jeff agreeably. "Remind her that she'll be saving a lot of arsenic."

Mrs. Lovelace was unconcerned. "As a matter of

fact I hadn't started dinner, no. I just finished cleaning the house. I had to stop at two, of course, for the Revival Hour. You'll find everything nice and clean when you come back. I've given it a good turning out. All, that is, except the master bedroom. I haven't done that yet. It was his room, you know, and—it's not really as though anyone was going to use it, is it?"

"If you don't feel like cleaning it, don't," Laurel advised.

Mrs. Lovelace's pallid voice bristled ever so slightly. "I am not one to shirk any duty, however irksome."

"I know you're not," said Laurel fervently. As she hung up the receiver, something mean in her mind said, *In fact, the more irksome the job is, the greater your feeling of virtue.*

When they returned to the house on the hill, with the green dregs of sunset beyond it, they found the living-room empty. As Laurel sat down in one of the big chairs she felt like an actor who has wandered onto a stage with the curtain up and not a line in her head.

André sat in a chair facing hers. Jeff and Woody drew up two more chairs so that the four of them were sitting in a circle around the cold fireplace. "Arsenic by accident," said André, the side of his head resting against one little hand, his eyes very alive in his thin, triangular face, "is rather hard to swallow." He grinned and sobered. "That's almost a joke, isn't it?"

"Almost," said Laurel.

"Murder," said Woody eagerly and engagingly, "seems to be committed so often for such very inadequate reasons. In stories there's usually the million-dollar will, or the rubies buried in the flowerpot. But actually, people kill people for rather simple reasons. Every murderer I have any accurate information about seems

to have been a simple person with a fixed idea. Look at
Bloody Mary. You imagine a dark and terrible creature
taking violent delight in cruelty and death. But an
authenticated portrait of her shows a meek and pale
little wisp of a woman, timidly holding out a rose. She
just believed very hard in Catholicism, that's all. So
the heads had to bend over the chopping block. A
simple soul with a fixed idea. Not a delusion, mind
you. Nothing tangled in the fringes of insanity. And
all the murderers I know much about were like that.
No perspective. They all were dwellers in a narrow
world, and sometimes without even knowing it another
person transgressed the rules of that narrow world. And
then woke up dead."

"You're breaking my heart," said Jeff. "I had always
hoped to meet one genuine Borgia before I died."

"Just before, that would be," said Laurel.

Woody ignored them, not impolitely, but because he
was so full of what he was saying. "The typical modern
murder—and I'll tell you about it because it so perfectly
illustrates what I've been saying—was committed by a
woman. She was an Oriental, the daughter of a mother
so poor that she had been raised on a river barge; only
the rich owned land. Because of her beauty, she became
the rough equivalent of the wife of a member of the
French consulate. That was a custom, for these men are
stationed half a world away from the Rue de la Paix for
years at a time. Finally, this particular consul was at
last called home to France. The wife wept and begged
him not to go; he would meet a woman of his own land
and never return. He explained his duty in the matter.
There was weeping and a tender parting, and the consul
died on the ship. Presumably he died of an obscure
intestinal ailment. Actually he died of the poison in
which his wife had soaked his favorite sweetmeats, her
parting gift. She was motivated, I believe, by two simple

reasons. First, she did not want another woman to have him. Second, the arrangements were such that she inherited much of his property. She lived quietly and nicely, I am told, and probably regretted losing him. His body was buried at sea."

"How do you know all this?" asked Laurel.

"I saw her buy the poison. I did not," Woody added, "know how she was going to use it.

"I saw her again last year in one of the most famous bars in Shanghai. She was sitting alone at a table at the far end of the room, wearing an emerald pendant. She had, I remember, a jeweled butterfly in her black hair. She looked rather tired, and her wide, high–cheek-boned face had in it no evil, no cruelty and no remorse." He added gravely, "The simple person, with no per-spective, living in a narrow world of her own." He cocked his head. "I think she made a mistake. I be-lieve he would have come back to her. Maybe—" he added—"maybe he does."

There was a scream, loud and sustained. It came from the floor below. The four of them leaped to their feet as though the scream had been a lash laid across their shoulders, and their footsteps as they went clattering down the stairs could have heralded an army.

They never could decide why, later, but they all headed for the Red Room. Mrs. Lovelace was backing out, her face in her hands, her shoulder blades almost breaking through her gray dress as she sobbed.

When they questioned her, she shook her head from side to side and only Laurel caught the words, "Under the bed!" muffled by those thin hands, those tears.

She went into the Red Room. The vacuum cleaner was standing at the foot of the bed, wheezing enor-mously. She clicked the switch near the handle, and the wheeze subsided into grateful silence. In fact, after the excitement of the day and the preceding excess of noise, it was the most silence Laurel had heard in some time. She raised the vermilion satin spread and peered into the square of darkness beneath the bed.

The great Dane was lying on its side, its legs stiff, its belly swollen, its head strained back. She did not have to lay her hand on its cold flank to know that it was dead.

CHAPTER ELEVEN

THE MONSTROUS AND THE HORRIBLE

"YES," said Dr. Day, "Mrs. Morrissey was quite correct in stating that there was no arsenic in any of the capsules." He hesitated. "There's a thought that does occur to me," he said. "I wonder if there might have been poison only in the capsule Mrs. Morrissey took." He shook his head. "Mathematically, though, that's not very probable. Because there were eleven capsules in the box I took to the laboratory for analysis. It would mean that, by a twelve-to-one chance, she took the single capsule containing arsenic."

"I agree," said Tuck. "It rather strains my credulity too."

As he rode toward the Los Angeles City Hall on the Sunset bus he wondered about a murderer bold enough to attempt two poisonings in 24 hours.

Woody tapped at Mrs. Lovelace's closed door, from behind which came the soothing sound of Negro voices singing, *Swing Low, Sweet Chariot.* The music was lowered. "What is it?" asked Mrs. Lovelace querulously.

"Could you tell us where a flashlight is? We think we'd like to look for the other dogs."

"In the garage," said Mrs. Lovelace, and turned up the radio: "*A ba-a-nd of an-gels comin' after me-eee—*"

They found the flashlight hanging on a hook directly in front of the long and shining hood of Falkoner's black car. As Woody reached up for it, Laurel heard an automobile approaching the house; the sound of its motor loudened, and then the nose of a gray Buick edged into the garage, the sound of its engine making huge echoes until Jim turned off the ignition. The car's doors opened simultaneously, and Jim and Tom got out. Tom squeezed his big body between the Cord and the Buick and made his way to Woody. "Whatcha doin'?"

"Someone's poisoned Pete. We're going to look for the other two dogs."

"Poisoned Pete," said Tom slowly.

"What's that?" asked Jim, making his way toward them as Tom had just done.

"Someone's poisoned Pete. He's under the bed in the Red Room. We want to look for the other two."

Jim looked at Woody. "Did you try calling them?"

"We don't know their names."

"Oh."

The six of them left the garage and went into the house. "I thought we might try the garden first," Woody said.

Jim went to the white door beside the view window and opened it onto the cool black night. Silently they filed down the outer stairs. Jim went to the edge of the terrace and cupped his hands to his mouth, letting out several piercing whistles, which were followed by complete silence except for the empty song of crickets. He called, "Champ! Playboy!" The faint hoot of a train somewhere in the San Fernando Valley answered his call.

Woody switched on the beam of the flashlight. "You'd better switch on the terrace lights," he said to Tom, who turned obediently.

The six lanterns above their heads blazed suddenly on. "Look," said Woody. Laurel's eyes followed his pointing finger and saw two round glass pie plates at the top of the steps leading down to the garden. The mound of meat in each was untouched.

The upper part of the sloping garden yielded nothing, so they moved, a compact group whose six pairs of eyes probed every shadow, to the lower end, where the light of the terrace did not reach. The inquiring beam of Woody's flashlight probed and paused, and Laurel could feel the big hulk of Jim treading on her heels, could hear the slow rhythm of his breathing.

Then the beam of yellow light they were following made a bright puddle on the high white wall at the end of the garden. Woody veered to the left toward a clump of oleander bushes, their pink blossoms pale in the artificial light.

They found one coach dog between the bushes and the white wall. His nose, pointed out from the flat spotted body, seemed to be smelling a low-blossoming pink flower. The eyes might have been half closed in ecstasy rather than in death.

Looking down at the dead dog, Laurel found herself thinking that the great Dane under the bed had possessed a certain majesty while this lank and spotted beast was as wistfully ridiculous as a dead harlequin.

That's what I'd have named them. Harlequin and Petrouchka instead of Champ and Playboy. And I'd have called the big dog Hamlet.

The thought just brushed her mind that the literal quality of the dead man's brain had revealed itself in the dull names he had given his dogs.

And then the physical aspect of the moment took swift possession of her. A group of silent shadows surrounding a pool of light, looking down out of six pairs of eyes at the spotted coach dog. Jim was beside her. She looked up at Jim.

His face, which she could just discern against the sky, was as impassive as it had been when she looked up at him for the first time, three deaths ago.

They found the second coach dog directly across the garden. Curiously, he had also chosen an oleander bush beside which to die, and he also seemed to be sniffing one of the wide pink flowers.

When Tuck opened the door of the Homicide Squad, Gufferty was talking with a small detective named Kern, who said, "No kiddin'? Say, it's weird!"

"Oh," said Gufferty, "so you decided to drop in?"

Kern turned and stood watching them expectantly.

"Nice to see you," said Gufferty.

"Nice to see *you*," said Tuck.

"You should drop in more often," said Gufferty. "*Where the hell have you been?*"

"Busy."

"You should drop around more often," Gufferty repeated. He grinned maliciously. "Because while you've been busy, *somebody poisoned the dogs!*"

"*What!*" said Tuck.

"All three of them," said Gufferty. "The girl found the first one under the bed. They realized they hadn't heard anything from the dogs all day, and the whole screwy household went looking for the other two. They found them behind a couple of bushes in the garden. A guy named Cornell talked with me and said he's seen poisoned dogs before, and that these have been poisoned." He leaned so far back in his swivel chair that he was almost reclining, and scratched his head. "You're going to have *fun*," he said somberly.

Laurel had been part of just such a scene many times before. A roomful of people, quieted by music, their bodies relaxed, their minds still and responsive. But tonight she knew that Mozart was being heard for another purpose than pure enjoyment. It was being half listened to by six people who needed the comfort of one another's presence, and who also needed an excuse for their silence. The music went on and on, exquisite harmony fading and growing louder there in the big bright room. She was glad to hear the door chimes sound. Jim stood up abruptly and moved swiftly across the soundless carpet to answer their summons.

Tuck looked even more weary to her than he had that morning. The flesh around his eyes was stained dark with fatigue, and the eyes themselves had sunk slightly into his head so that they caught no light whatever.

Everyone in the room seemed to come alive. Jeff jumped to his feet, André straightened on the hassock beside the fireplace, and Tom, who had been lying on his belly before the hearth, sat up rubbing his eyes with first one fist and then the other so that he was watching Tuck all the while. The vacant, almost brooding look left Woody's face, and he watched Tuck too. Laurel saw that Jim, who was standing behind Tuck, had to look up at him just a little, which vaguely pleased her.

"I want to see those dogs," Tuck said.

Jim led him to the white door, and they went down the outer stairs together.

When Tuck returned, he asked, "Who put that meat out on the terrace?"

"Mrs. Lovelace, I suppose," said Jim.

"Who fed them last night?"

"I guess I did," said Jim.

"When?"

"Just a little while before Tom and me left. About six o'clock."

Tuck looked at him with those tired eyes.

Jim rubbed one ear as though to stimulate his memory. "Let's see, Mrs. Lovelace was gone. She was the one that mostly fed them. Then I walked them. Last night I saw them playing in the garden, and that reminded me it was Mrs. Lovelace's day off and I had to feed them. So I went into the kitchen. Mrs. Lovelace had the meat all ready in the icebox—on the two glass plates. One for the spotted dogs, and one for Pete."

"Hamburger, the same as tonight?"

"Yeah. I took the two plates and put them down at the top of the steps and whistled and they came running and I left them there eating their heads off."

An apt figure of speech, thought Tuck. He said, "Did you see them alive at any time after that?"

Jim thought. "No. Because when Tom and I got back from the show it was late, like I told you, and we went to bed. And the next morning we got up and after we dressed we went straight up to the kitchen to start getting breakfast, and then Miss Byrd screamed and we went down and found Mr. Falkoner was dead, and after that we didn't think much about the dogs."

Tuck looked around at the attentive faces. "Did any of you see the dogs alive after you left the house last night?"

They all shook their heads.

"Oh," said Tuck. "That reminds me." He turned to André. "There are three cars here. Miss Byrd, Mr. Prince, and Mr. Cornell used one. Tom and Jim used one. And Mr. Falkoner used one. How did you leave here last night?"

"I walked." André Viaud added, a little defensively, "I like to walk."

"All right," said Tuck. He turned back to Jim. "Do you have any idea how the great Dane got under the bed?"

Jim turned to Tom. "Did you lock the door to the terrace like I told you?"

"I forgot."

Jim looked at Tuck. "Unless Mr. Falkoner locked it before he left, it was open all evening."

"Was it shut when you and Tom returned?"

"Yeah. So Mr. Falkoner must have shut it. Maybe

before he left, or maybe after he got back and was undressing to go to bed."

"Now I'd like to talk to the cook," said Tuck.

"I'll take you down to her room," Jim offered.

Laurel stood up. "Please, Mr. Tuck, I have a friend in Los Angeles who'd love to have me visit her. Couldn't I—?"

"Not yet," said Tuck.

Mrs. Lovelace opened her door a crack. When she saw Tuck she opened it wider. "Yes?" she asked, rather tremulously.

"I have a few questions, Mrs. Lovelace. May I come in?"

She darted a quick look around the room, and then opened the door to almost its full extent.

"Thanks," Tuck said to Jim, who nodded and went upstairs.

Mrs. Lovelace had been sitting in a low maple rocker beside a small radio. She had, he saw, been darning a lisle stocking; on seeing him glance at it, she went swiftly over and wrapped it with quick modesty around the darning egg that bulged in the toe.

"When did you buy the meat that Jim fed to the dogs last night?"

"Jim drove me to the market the day before. Wednesday morning that would be. Before I went to my sister's on Thursday afternoon, I took it out of the butcher paper and divided it out onto the two plates and put them on the bottom shelf of the icebox."

"Then it was wrapped in its original paper from Wednesday morning until Thursday afternoon?"

"Oh, no. You never leave meat in paper. When I put the groceries away Wednesday morning, I unwrapped the meat and put it in a big bowl and covered it with wax paper."

"When you divided it into two portions on Thursday afternoon, did you notice anything odd about it? Had it been disturbed?"

"Oh, there was something odd about it, all right. There was a *great deal* of suet in it. I know why. That butcher knows it's for dogs. I am convinced he grinds it specially, and grinds a great deal of suet in with it, charging me, of course, the regular price. Butchers are not to be trusted. Their profession callouses them."

"Suet is white, isn't it?"

"Yes." She looked up at Tuck, and he decided that she had eyes that matched her voice, pale and monotonous eyes. "Mr. Tuck, I want to leave this place."

"You're not alone there. I'll let you know just as soon as it's possible."

"If I could do any *good*," she said, almost fiercely, "if I could spread any *light*. And besides, my salary is paid up to and including today."

"I'm really sorry," said Tuck. "Stick it out a little longer, will you?"

Mrs. Lovelace straightened her thin shoulders in their gray rayon dress. "Very well," she said.

"And tell me one thing more. Was the milk, and Mr. Falkoner's buttermilk, delivered at the door, or did you buy it when you did the other marketing?"

"I bought it. No milk company in the world would send a truck clear up here for one delivery."

"And Mr. Falkoner's buttermilk—the buttermilk he drank on Thursday evening sometime—did you buy that on Wednesday when you bought the dogs' meat?"

"Yes," said Mrs. Lovelace.

Tuck stood winding his alarm clock. As he wound, his tired brain remembered how a long time ago his strong fingers had wound a clock too tightly and how something had clicked sharply inside, and how the ticking had stopped abruptly, how the clock had gone dead in his hands.

He thought that the murderer might be somewhat like that clock. The strong hands of circumstance wound and wound too tightly, and inside something snapped, and time stopped while murder was done.

Clocks that do that sometimes go again, he thought. *And I guess with people, too, after the violent reaction has taken place, the hands can be made to turn, and no one looking at the bland and usual face could guess that there were some hours not a part of the smooth continuum of hours and days and years.*

After Laurel turned out the light, her room was at first black with a bold patch of moonlight under the closed window, but gradually the shapes of furniture emerged from the darkness around her.

Now why, she wondered, should the death of three dogs be more horrible than the death of a man? Why was I shocked and yet not deeply moved by Falkoner's death, and then knocked for a loop by the dog under the bed? And then the dogs by the pink oleander bushes?

I know why. Rage against another human being is understandable. Rage that extends to his dogs is monstrous. I see where this idea is leading.

But wait. Could the dogs have been poisoned by accident? By eating whatever it was that killed Falkoner? No. Dogs aren't vegetarians. So it's not likely that they were killed by accident by the person who planned only to kill Falkoner. And conversely, he couldn't have been accidentally poisoned by a crank who wanted only to kill the dogs. And then there's Denise Morrissey, too.

I wonder how long it takes for a dog to die of poison? Probably a shorter time than it takes a man. Smaller. Not so far for the poison to travel before it reaches the

*place where the death begins. That's silly. It's probably
about as far to a dog's small intestines as to a man's.
Maybe Woody will know. I'll ask him in the morning.
I must ask him how he happened to be so sure.*

The coroner's men looked very funny, bending over
to see the dog under the bed. They were so businesslike about carrying the dogs out that I suspect they
were astounded, but considered it a professional lapse
to show it. I wonder what the coroner will think. Maybe
he'll complain, "My job is to investigate for the cause
of the death of a human cadaver. Nothing was said
about dogs. At dogs I draw the line."

She giggled in the darkness, and was startled at the
sound. The giggle sounded like the giggle of a maniac.

*But he needn't have been crazy, the murderer. Only
very full of hate. I wish I'd eaten my dinner. I could go
up to the kitchen and fix a piece of bread and butter.
And a glass of milk.*

She thought of going through the still dark house,
with breathers behind each door, and behind one door
one person hearing her pass, then holding his breath with
the momentary notion that she was some nemesis come
in the night to do unto him what he had done.

*How silly! The only people in the house are Jeff,
whom I've known for four years, and who would detour
rather than step on a bug, and Woody, bless his heart,
and Mrs. Lovelace, who probably thinks that Falkoner
was killed by a just God not too proud to use arsenic,
and André. And probably Jim and Tom. They couldn't*
possibly *sleep one each side of that empty cot.*

Why am I afraid?

*This is a house on a hill above Hollywood, and a
good clean wind is coming in from the Pacific Ocean,
and down in the city the lights are bright, and some
people are asleep and some people are dancing. There
is no more horror in this house than there is down there*

in the city, and I am not afraid.

Horror is the thing you are afraid of for fear that it might be there. You could do a rather neat paper on the evolution of the horrible. In Rome, stars fell and wolves ran through the streets when the gods were planning something queer. And in the Middle Ages there were the revenants. The ones who came back in human flesh and blood. They had a pale green tinge. And then, with more sophistication, the corpse that walked could no longer be believed in, and so entered the ectoplasmic ghosts. You put your hand out to touch one, and touched the wall. And now we don't believe in them any more. Psychology has given us something worse. We've got the diseased and twisted mind looking out of eyes like any other eyes. The mind that may at any moment prompt the hands it governs to commit any horror. That's worse than the revenants were. That's worse than the lady in white who walked the castle halls at the stroke of twelve.

But the person who killed Falkoner was not necessarily insane. Not at all. Because if Harvers was telling the truth, Falkoner was a wrong 'un. But the dogs? The hollow feeling in her stomach intensified.

Resolutely she flung back the covers, shoved her feet into her slippers, and drew on her robe. The key snicked loudly as she unlocked her door. She realized that never before coming to live in this house had she ever locked her door at night.

The hall was black and cold. No light showed under the other doors. On reaching the foot of the stairs she clicked the switch that turned on the light in the upper hall, and went up to the kitchen. Seeing its blue-and-white commonplaceness was no comfort. For again she saw Tom with the carving knife.

Returning to her room, she locked her door after her, becoming at once irritably aware that after the cool airiness of the silent house her small room was fusty and airless. She pattered over to the closed and latched casement window, and pushed both halves out wide into the moonlit night. Once again her eyes fell on the three cots below the outer staircase. She was shocked to see Tom and Jim lying one on each side of the empty cot in the middle.

Tom was lying on his stomach, the rumpled back of his head turned toward her. Jim was lying on his back, in the nearest cot. She saw that his pale eyes were open, staring up at the round moon riding high in the western sky.

A pang of excited terror burst in her chest. *I must not scream, she told herself wildly. I found a man dead this morning and screamed. I must not scream.*

And then, like the eyes of some mechanical toy, Jim's eyes turned slowly in his head and met her own.

TUCK was pouring his third cup of breakfast coffee when the doorbell rang. Knowing Brigit, he had expected the doorbell to ring, and the gnawing of the expectation had somewhat dimmed his appreciation of Sibelius's Second Symphony.

He opened his front door onto Brigit, Froody and Mr. Gonzales's small fat dog, backed by the green hill and its stubby black oil wells. Tuck did not let Mr. Gonzales's dog in, knowing from experience that his paws would be thick with the oil that Mr. Gonzales's well pumped up day and night, providing the wherewithal for dogs and children and wine.

"Music?" asked Brigit doubtfully, looking over at Tuck's radio-phonograph.

"Yes."

"This early in the morning?"

"It's never too early for music. Never too late . . . How are your mumps, Froody?"

Froody pointed with both fat forefingers at his somewhat swollen jowels. His myopic eyes, the color of gooseberries, were gloomy and resigned. "At any age," he mourned, "it's funny."

Tuck opened his mouth to speak, but Froody implored his silence with a plump palm. "No. Don't try to make me feel better. When I phoned Gufferty last week what was the matter, I heard him say 'Froody has the mumps, folks.' I heard them laugh." Froody thought for a moment and then assayed an unconvincing smile. " 'Froody has the mumps.' It *is* funny."

"At your age they can be very serious," Brigit said.

Froody regarded her doubtfully. "You're not just saying that to make me feel good?"

"I know someone who was forty-nine and got mumps and died of them," stated Brigit.

"Honest?" asked Froody. He was visibly cheered.

"I got about twenty names and addresses last night," Brigit said to Tuck. "Two of them are obviously phonies. No one could possibly be named Murgatroyd Anstruther, or Jacqueline Burpee. I keep asking myself, is that last one a name, or a condition?"

"Are you on this case too, Froody?" Tuck asked.

Brigit had the grace to look a trifle guilty.

"I guess, so. Miss Estees phoned me this morning and told me you needed me, so I phoned Gufferty and told him I had the doc's O. K., so here I am."

"I'm glad to see you," Tuck said, "because with both of you going through the poison books, we'll get there twice as fast."

Brigit looked glum.

"If," said Froody, "this guy bought the poison, in the last two weeks, in this town."

"Exactly."

"Of course," said Froody judicially, thoroughly at home with this particular problem, "he probably signed a fake name, which means that Miss Estees and I will have to check on all the addresses."

Brigit looked still glummer.

"But," said Tuck, "cover everything in or near Hollywood first. I've found something funny about this business of buying poison. You get a stupid guy, and he'll sign John Doe every time. You get a smart guy, and he'll figure it out something like this: 'The police have experts who can compare handwriting and find similarities regardless of disguise. So if I sign a fake name, I'm admitting my guilt. If I sign my own name, that will be a talking point for the innocence of my motive in buying

the poison.' So then they make up some story about the
rats in the attic, and sign their own name in the poison
book."

"Right," said Froody wisely.

Tuck turned to Brigit. "Froody can teach you a lot
you'll never learn from me. You're lucky that he's in on
this with you."

"I'd figure that he'd take on the poison-book detail,
and that you'd use me some other way," said Brigit.

"Brigit," said Tuck, "in spite of the fact that your
dad was a cop, you've decided that there's glamour in
the job of being a detective. Now is a good time for
you to learn that there isn't. Although," he added,
"this case is a bit different. Did Gufferty tell you that
it looks as though the murderer poisoned Falkoner's
three dogs?"

Brigit gave a banshee's wail.

Mrs. Callender again opened the door of the old
house in St. James Place. She had on the same dark
dress and her eyes were still mournful.

"Is Miss Callender at home?" Tuck asked.

"She's not up yet," said Mrs. Callender dimly.

"I'll wait," said Tuck.

Mrs. Callender made a dignified gesture at a hard,
tall-backed, solid mahogany chair to the left of the
door, and plodded up the wide staircase which swept
to the second floor from the center of the big hall.

Tuck had fallen to counting the stalks of pussy-willow
spraying forlornly from the mouth of a huge dull brass
vase atop a very small teakwood taboret in one corner,
when a young woman in red appeared at the head of the
stairs. She descended slowly, the fingers of one long
hand on the dark banister. When she reached him, she
extended her hand. "I'm Rita Callender. I know wny
you want to see me. Let's go into the living-room."

The living-room was a drawing-room. Dull green carpet, crystal chandeliers, a huge black piano, Louis Quinze furniture. Rita Callender was so vividly out of place against that background that Tuck had the feeling for a moment that she, like himself, was a visitor in the house.

"Mother," she said, "tells me that my dress is most unsuitable. With mother, when someone's dead, you make all the gestures." She tipped her head at him. "I'm wearing red because it was his favorite color. Sentimental of me, isn't it?"

Tuck realized that she was young, for all the stains of last night's revelry under her eyes. He realized that he would learn far more from a monologue than from any questions he might put. But there were a few questions he had to ask.

"I am trying to get the timetable straight," he said. "At what time did you and Mrs. Morrissey leave Mr. Falkoner's house, the day before he died?"

"Five-thirty, I should say. I'm not too sure."

"And where did you go?"

"To the Beachcomber's for dinner. I wanted to go home to change, but Denise said it would take too long, so I just put on my coat. I had it in the car."

"And you went straight to the Beachcomber's?"

"Yes."

"And where did you go after that?"

"Denise went home. She looked dead. I went home too. I do that one or two nights a week to keep mother happy."

"And what time was it when you yourself arrived at Falkoner's Wednesday afternoon?"

"Four-ish."

"Before Miss Byrd came up to the living-room, did anyone else do so?"

"No. Mrs. Lovelace let me in. When she said Earl

wasn't in, I said I'd wait awhile in case he might come home. She went back to the kitchen and I went into the living-room."

"And Mrs. Lovelace remained in the kitchen?"

"I guess so."

"What were your relations with Mr. Falkoner?"

She gave a hard laugh. "That phrase is wonderful. Very suggestive. There weren't any 'relations,' Mr. Tuck."

"I understand that you were very fond of him."

"Fond? No, I wasn't fond. I was nuts about the guy."

"Did he reciprocate?"

"No."

"I wonder why?"

"So do I. I've made a guess. Do you want to hear it?"

"Sure."

"It begins with 'There comes a time in every young man's life—'. But there does, I think. It's when he reaches physical and mental maturity. And the person he happens to be in love with then, or even nearly so, he marries. But if a man is going places, so that a wife would be a responsibility which might keep him from his goal, there are some men who are hard enough to put love aside. And then their time of vulnerability passes, and they freeze into bachelors, and think they've been pretty smart."

"How old are you?" asked Tuck.

"Twenty-five. In years, that is."

"So you think that Falkoner had become impervious to woman?"

"Oh, that's only part of it. Don't forget that he was a vegetarian."

Tuck blinked.

"He abstained," said Rita. "His philosophy of life,

if you could call it that, was something very like the good old 'sound mind in a sound body.' I think his plan was to compensate for his lack of formal education by building up a healthy torso."

Tuck laughed.

"It's not funny," said Rita. "It's rather sad."

Tuck decided that he wanted her to talk some more. "You seem to have a peculiar trait, for a woman. Most women build the men they love quite away from the raw material. You seem to have seen the man as he really was."

"Psychology did that for me. I know all the little tricks our minds play on us. I know that 'love' is largely a rationalization of a very simple urge. I know a lot." Her eyes were bright with tears. "I know myself," she said. "I know myself quite well. I'm a clever young woman, freed from the old taboos. I'm as useless as a member of the French aristocracy because I inherited a little money and half of a house. I've never channeled my energies. I probably never will. In six months Earl Falkoner will be a face I'll remember suddenly sometimes when I'm falling asleep. Every once in while, just as I'm going to sleep he'll be walking toward me, real, three-dimensional. And I'll be sick with love for him, but in the morning I'll have lunch with someone else."

This has gone far enough, Tuck thought. "Do you have any idea, any idea at all, why Falkoner was murdered, or who did it?"

Rita nodded briskly. "Yes. I think Denise Morrissey did."

"Why?"

"I've found out things about Denise. 'Know your enemy.' I met her when I first saw Falkoner, a year ago at someone's party. The minute I saw Falkoner, he interested me. And I saw this blond woman with him who had once been prettier, and I didn't worry much. I did my little song and dance for Earl, and got him invited to a couple of parties friends of mine were giving. He wasn't interested. Then I met Ruth De Lisle, and took her to lunch a few times, and she asked me to dinner several times, and Falkoner was there with Denise. So I asked Ruth about her.

"When she was nineteen she left her home town— I think it was Pomona, or one of those other California small towns—and went to San Francisco, where she got a job as a secretary for Dun and Bradstreet. Why? So that she could have at her fingertips the financial status of any man she might meet."

"That's a guess, isn't it?" asked Tuck mildly.

"Not entirely," said Rita. "Anyway, she finally met Joel Morrissey a clever, ugly, rich little producer, and married him. She's about forty now, Mr. Tuck. She's managed without love this far, but she's at a dangerous age. I think she was in love with Falkoner. I think she found he didn't give a hoot about her. I think she killed him for it."

"Whew!"

"I think she took something a good deal short of a fatal dose of poison in order to point suspicion away from herself."

"You don't like her much, do you?"

"No. She stands for all the things I detest. Bridge. Nice little dinner parties. Lunch at Bullock's Wilshire, with everyone cooing over the dresses as the models pass by. Marriage for security. One Alexander or a champagne cocktail instead of three Scotch ands."

"Why did Falkoner apparently like her so?"

"For just the reason he didn't take to me. She has all the surface qualities of a lady. If there are any others, Yes, I guess there are. A lady fools herself into believing that she's not an animal at all, but something created to wear perfume and clothes. A lady 'gives' herself to a man, even if she happens to have married him. She 'gives' herself, in return, of course, for room, board, clothes, furs, jewelry, a car and a nice allowance."

"And I take that you don't consider yourself a lady?"

"Not by a long shot," said Rita.

"How about Thursday night? What did you do?"

"Just a quiet evening at home. Oh, I left the house about eight and took some books back to the library, and stopped at a bar for a drink on the way back."

"And when did you learn that Falkoner was dead?"

"Friday after lunch. Ruth De Lisle had phoned me for the first time in ages and ages that morning to tell me about Denise being poisoned. I don't know why, but I formed the impression that it was one of those medicine-cabinet accidents—reaching for the wrong bottle, you know. But after I learned that Earl was dead, I saw the whole picture. I went on with a lad to meet some people. I went on out of desperation. I was afraid to be alone. And quite suddenly, just as I raised a glass to my lips, I saw the whole thing. Denise. All the Denises of the world, for whom life is so smooth. And one thing that didn't come to her, when she wanted it badly." Her white face was brooding, her eyes dark with her thoughts.

Tuck watched her. Then he said, "Miss Callender, when you and Mrs. Morrissey were at dinner on Wednesday evening, did she tell you that she was thinking of marrying Mr. Falkoner?"

Rita's head jerked up. "No. No, she didn't."

On his way to The Towers, Tuck stopped and telephoned Dr. Day at his office. "I'm interested in Mrs. Morrissey's poisoning again. It was a fatal dose?"

"It was."

"You'll see exactly the meaning behind this question.

Could Mrs. Morrissey have given herself a fatal dose of arsenic, relying on her knowledge that you lived in the same apartment house to pull her out of it? Or did she know you lived there too?"

"She knew. In fact, she and my wife have been acquaintances for several months."

"I see."

"But I am certain that she did not poison herself—for whatever reason you may have in mind—and rely on my availability to keep her from dying. Because on Thursday nights I am always on duty at the County Hospital until the early hours of the morning."

"And Mrs. Morrissey knew this?"

"Certainly. She and my wife usually spent that evening together, for the very reason that I couldn't be at home to keep my wife company."

"I see."

"It was by an absolute, unforeseeable fluke that I happened to come home when I did this Thursday. Even my wife didn't expect me. It probably won't happen again for ten years."

"Well, thanks a lot."

"Furthermore, no one but a fool would try to play tricks with poison. And a mighty careless fool at that. Mrs. Morrissey's not a fool. She's a sensible woman of forty, not a hysterical girl."

"I agree with you," said Tuck. "Thanks again."

When Mrs. Morrissey opened the door of her apartment, she had a dark blue hat on. She opened the door wider to let him in. "If you had something you were planning to do, I could come back later," Tuck offered.

"That's not at all necessary. I was only going shopping." Her voice wavered, but her eyes remained steady. "I haven't a thing black except one dinner dress. . . . What did you wish to see me about?" she asked, when they were seated exactly as they had been the night before.

"I'd like to know if you have any ideas about how you came to be poisoned."

She thought for a long moment, and then said, "Yes, I have." She looked steadily at him. He noticed that she was less pallid than she had been, or else her skillfully applied make-up camouflaged the fact.

"Last night, of course, I was too utterly horrified about Earl's death to think at all clearly. I'm still horrified about it, and I think I shall always be. But I find that I can think today. Of course, the outstanding thing about it all is that someone tried to kill me too, isn't it? I mean, Mr. Tuck, I couldn't have accidentally swallowed that poison. There were only two people who had an opportunity to kill me. Ruth De Lisle and Rita Callender. Ruth is of course out. I've known her for years and we're very fond of each other. She wouldn't do a thing like that to anyone, but certainly not to me. But Rita. Really, Mr. Tuck, that woman amazes me. She's been throwing herself at Earl for almost a year now, and women who throw themselves at men just aren't sound to begin with. And she drinks. Oh, how she drinks! I saw her once—her eyes were all shiny and horrible and she looked capable of anything.

"I'm not at all prudish about drinking, don't misunderstand me. I have always thought that Earl carried it too far, and I've told him so. But women can't drink, Mr. Tuck. I was young in the twenties when everyone carried a flask. One of the first times I went out with a man in a big city I saw a woman drunk. Not just tipsy, but *drunk*. I made up my mind that I would never, never look like that.

"However, that's not really very much to the point, is it? What I'm getting at is this: Rita was quite tight when we had dinner together Wednesday night. That was really the only reason I went. I was rather afraid that she might make some sort of a scene if I absolutely refused, although I tried to, goodness knows.

"Now why in the world she'd have arsenic with her, I don't know, Mr. Tuck. You'll have to figure that out for yourself. But when we were sitting opposite each other there at that little table at the Beachcomber's, I suddenly realized that she hated me. The boy came, and she ordered a drink before dinner. I refused. That was absolutely all. She just sat there looking at me and I realized that she hated me. It had nothing to do with Earl. She hated me, as a separate person. It was a very shocking moment.

"When the coffee came I left the table for a few minutes. As I look back, Mr. Tuck, *there was something very strange about the taste of that coffee*," she whispered.

"I see," said Tuck.

"Do you?" asked Denise, peering into his eyes. "Please don't think me horrible for saying such things. I have forced myself to think that after all the basic thing is that Earl is dead, and the person who killed him should be brought to justice."

"If I told you that his three dogs have been killed too, would you still suspect Rita?"

"Oh!" said Denise. Her hand went to her opened lips. "Oh, that's dreadful!" She frowned a little. "Yes. I think I would. I think that she drank too much and went crazy, and wanted to hurt everything that Earl cared for. Although," she added, "I must admit that he wasn't deeply attached to the dogs." She thought again. "But then Rita needn't have known that, need she?"

"She did know that he was fond of you, though."

"Yes. That really must have been the basis for her dislike to me. No one could possibly hate a person like me that much."

"Did you tell Rita that you and Mr. Falkoner were going to get married?"

She looked startled. "No. Only Ruth. Did she tell you? It wasn't that definite, really, but I *had* been thinking of it." She looked down abruptly at her lap. "I was very fond of him. I understood him. His life had been something like mine—born in a small town and wanting more. I felt that together we might be rather happy. If that's all, could you go now, please? I'm going to cry again."

The ladies, God bless 'em, thought Tuck, as he rode down in the honey-colored elevator. *Not catting, those two. No, worse than that. They both were quite sure they were telling the truth.*

He phoned the medical examiner. "Is it possible for a person to drink to excess, commit a rash act or acts while the brain is under the influence of alcohol, and wake up with no remembrance of what he did? Not an inkling? None at all?"

"That depends. It's possible, yes. But I would say that the person would have to have unusual tolerance to alcohol in order to drink and retain enough to cause the complete amnesia you speak of. A person with no abnormal tolerance might commit the rash act, all right, but would find himself face to face with it the next morning, along with his hangover."

"Thanks a lot. And switch me to the laboratory, will you?"

"And say, in case you're still interested, those dogs that came in last night were all given a stiff dose of arsenic. In fact, an incredibly stiff dose. About three times the minimum lethal dose."

"That's good," Tuck said. "I was half afraid it would turn out to be curare."

"Yes," said the precise voice of the police chemist, "we've got the report ready. It's on its way to your office now. To brief it, absolutely nothing you sent us contained the slightest trace of arsenic or any other poison."

So that reflected Tuck, *leaves the buttermilk.* He wondered if he were stretching a point in glimpsing for a flicker of time, the faint suggestion of a drunken, irrational irony implicit in the act of killing a teetotaler by means of poisoned buttermilk.

CHAPTER THIRTEEN
THIS SOWING OF DEATH

TUCK looked at the drying bitten sandwich. He looked at the cold pool of coffee in the bottom of the cylindrical cardboard container. He stood up and walked to the circular expanse of windows which walled in the tower of the City Hall. He stood at a northeast window, looking out across the wide flat expanse of city, sharp in the white winter sunlight, to the low blue hills above Hollywood.

Nothing fits, he thought. *Every theory comes finally smack up against the fact that no one had the physical and psychological opportunity to poison Denise Morrissey, and kill Falkoner and the dogs.*

"Hello, there!" said Brigit's voice.

He turned and faced her and Froody across the huge model of downtown Los Angeles which had adorned the center of the tower for a long time, and whose purpose had always eluded him.

" 'Hello, there,' " he said, "has always got under my skin somehow, along with 'What do you know?' "

"The best bet," said Froody, "is this 'Taps for Rats.' " He drew a small notebook from his pocket and read, "Sixty-two percent arsenic trioxide, finely powdered." He returned the notebook to his pocket. "There's not much medical use for arsenic, they tell me. Too toxic."

"How are you coming with the poison registers?"

"Slowly. Miss Estees took the west end of Hollywood, I took the east, and we'll meet at about Hollywood and Vine in a day or so. How are *you* coming?"

"This case," stated Tuck, "is full of cul-de-sacs."

"Beg pardon?" asked Froody.

"Dead ends."

"Let's have it," said Brigit, and added, "You sound awfully low." She sat on the north end of Elysian Park and swung one leg. "I see you had lunch the other side of the tracks," she said, pointing at his sandwich and coffee cup, just east of Union Station.

Tuck grinned feebly.

Brigit's eyes were very kind. "Come on. Tell us all about it. It'll make you feel better. And maybe we can help."

Froody planted one elbow beside Tuck's coffee cup and watched him hopefully, his plump chin in his plump hand.

Tuck walked toward them, thinking, "I have always distrusted the ease with which, in a murder case which presents bizarre angles, the brain leaps toward the conclusion of insanity. But the three dogs defeat me. The incredible malignancy behind their murder is not sane. I've tried to discover a means by which they could have been poisoned accidentally. The best I could do along that line was that maybe someone poisoned their meat thinking it was Jim's and Tom's. But then you get a murderer who sets out to kill a man and his lady friend and his two bodyguards. Which isn't much of an improvement over a murderer who kills a man and his lady friend and his dogs.

"There were just two people who had the opportunity to kill Falkoner—Denise Morrissey and the dogs. Rita Callender could have poisoned the dogs' meat and the buttermilk—the lab says everything we brought from the house is uncontaminated—before Laurel Byrd came upstairs and found her listening to *Rhapsody in Blue.* And that's definite, because I questioned Mrs. Lovelace this morning and she admitted having been absent from the kitchen for fifteen minutes after Rita arrived. She went downstairs to listen to a radio program called

The Drums of Faith. Callender, she says, may or may not have seen her go through the entrance hall to the stairs. And Callender could have poisoned Mrs. Morrissey's coffee at dinner—in fact, Mrs. Morrissey thinks she did. So much for the physical opportunity. But you know as well as I that beyond the physical opportunity lies the problem of what I always think of as psychological opportunity. There are certain people who can commit certain acts, and others who can't. And a normal person can't kill a man and a woman and three dogs. I don't have to elaborate that—the act speaks for itself."

"A strictly normal person can't kill anybody," said Brigit.

"That is a generality which has been much discussed, and leads into the realm of criminal insanity. But any number of alienists don't agree with you. Certain temperaments, under certain conditions, are quite capable of murder, and are quite sane while committing it. But not this murder."

"I agree," said Froody.

"Good," said Tuck. "Now, having granted Rita Callender the physical opportunity for committing this crime, and using as a general motive her self-admitted and frustrated to-the-devil infatuation for Falkoner, let's take a look at the psychological opportunity. In other words, is her mentality—or rather, what we know of it— congruous with what we might as well get gaudy and call wholesale slaughter?"

"She drank," pounced Brigit.

"Ah," Tuck told her, "you are now entering blind alley number one. She drank. To excess. She also quite honestly—and you'll have to take my word for this—she quite honestly believes that Denise Morrissey killed Falkoner. Which means what? Which means that, unless I've become an old fuddy-duddy and have completely lost my flair for smelling a lie, she either didn't kill Falkoner, et cetera, *or has no recollection of having done so!"*

"If she was drunk enough—" Brigit began eagerly.

"Exactly. I talked with the medical examiner. **A** retroactive amnesia can result from excessive absorption of alcohol, providing the victim of the amnesia is capable of holding a lot of drinks, of which Miss Callender, by all reports, is very capable. So I talked with Miss Bryd this morning too. I asked her just how drunk she believed Miss Callender to have been on Wednesday afternoon. These are her exact words: 'Well, I could smell whisky on her breath. But she was perfectly lucid. She didn't stagger. I would say that the only mental effect she showed was in being perhaps a trifle wrought up emotionally.'"

"I'm beginning to see what you mean," said Brigit.

"Cornell and Prince said in effect the same thing. She left Falkoner's at the same time as Mrs. Morrissey, who followed her car down the hill. They had dinner together. Rita had one drink before dinner. Yet, if she poisoned Mrs. Morrissey at all, she must have done so while they ate dinner. But she was not drunk at that time. Even granting that she lied about going home after dinner—her mother doesn't know what time she came in—and got roaring, blind, crazy drunk, she wasn't in that state at the time when she had the only opportunity of which we know to poison Falkoner's buttermilk, the dogs' meat and Mrs. Morrissey. In other words, she had the physical opportunity, but as far as our knowledge goes, not the psychological one.

"The only other person who had an opportunity to kill Mrs. Morrissey was Ruth De Lisle. Providing that you don't balk at poisoned sherry. Furthermore, there is not a remote possibility that Falkoner was blackmailing her, although neither of them probably called it by that plain name. In other words, she was nuts about him—the man must have been a lot more charming alive than dead—indiscreetly gave him a large check, more discreetly gave him the next sum in cash. Upon learning that Wednesday afternoon that her old chum Denise was going to marry him, she slipped Denise a very final mickey and, as soon as she had finished eating dinner across the table from her husband, dashed up to Falkoner's, poisoned him and his dogs and arrived home in time to greet her dear friend's son, Woody Cornell, whom she rather dramatically warned to leave Falkoner's house, presumably because she had good reason to believe the police would be shuffling around looking for a suspect within twenty-four hours."

"You're corning it," objected Brigit. "Remember that your whole theory depends upon the fact that she was mad enough about Falkoner to betray her husband for him. That's the sort of love, I think, which is the most jealous kind. Having stooped so low for love, a woman kind of hates to lose it."

"In that case, we know nothing at all of the real Ruth De Lisle. We've seen the shallow picture she's hung over her real depths—in which lie a powerful capacity for love and hatred."

"And who would have a better idea than you of the real woman? Her husband! Does he suspect her of something not strictly kosher? Not much, he doesn't!"

"And then, of course, there's Harold De Lisle," said Tuck. "When his wife went to town after dinner for the wedding present—her story—he also could have left the house. Thursday night, you see. Their servants were out. Each of them has a car. He might have phoned Falkoner, intending to give him hell, found no one at home, got the mad idea of getting into the house somehow—and anyone who knew about that flimsy French door leading onto the terrace wouldn't have had much trouble, providing he could climb a four-foot wall—"

"And the French door was probably open, anyway," Brigit interpolated.

"Yes, there's even that. So, armed with arsenic, he drives to the empty house of the man who has debauched his wife and poisons his buttermilk and the dogs' meat. A vindictive frenzy. But—*why the devil would he poison Denise?*"

"Wait a minute!" said Brigit. "Could he have been having an affair with Denise, while his wife was having one with Falkoner? Maybe it grew out of that. Maybe, on learning of his wife and Falkoner, he decided that two could play that game, developed a flirtation with Denise until in the end she really possessed him. So then, learning that she is calmly considering marrying not only someone else, but his wife's lover, he— Tell me quick—who got the sherry Mrs. Morrissey drank?"

"He did. From the wine cellar."

"Ho! All right. And then, having started, he carried on to the bitter end. He gave himself over to a cold sort of berserkness and killed the lover too!"

"You've got a nice plot there," said Tuck admiringly.

"You mean you don't think it could happen?"

"I mean I'll have to find if, when and where he got the arsenic before I believe your theory. Well, there we are. We've covered everyone who could have killed Falkoner and his dogs, and poisoned Denise Morrissey. And it's claptrap!"

"Claptrap?" asked Froody.

Tuck found his arms wide in a gesture of wild hopelessness. "I don't believe it! I can't believe it! None of it ever happened in this world. Falkoner, yes. I can quite easily believe in a woman who killed a man, maybe her lover, because he demanded money from her and then decided to marry her old friend. I can believe in a husband going in a quiet and deadly way about poisoning his wife's lover. I can imagine a neurotic and useless young woman getting drunk and poisoning an older man who wouldn't look twice at her. I can believe any one of those. But it's this—this sowing about of death I can't believe in!"

Froody straightened. "You know what would help?" he asked, solicitously. "If you knew who bought some arsenic." He turned to Brigit. "Come on."

"I'm coming too," said Tuck, starting with them for the door. Then he stopped abruptly. "No, I won't. I'll start getting answers to some questions that bother me."

"What questions?" asked Brigit.

Tuck opened his black notebook, and read:

1. *Why did Falkoner have two bodyguards?*

2. *Was he afraid of someone? Who?*

3. *Does this have anything to do with his living in an isolated house?*

4. *Why was André living there?*

5. *Was Ruth De Lisle's story about the thousand dollars true?*

6. *Why were the dogs killed?*

"Wait!" commanded Brigit. "I just got an idea! Maybe the dogs were killed purely for purposes of confusion. I mean, maybe the murderer saw that they would lead you into a blind alley." She raised her shoulders in a quick shiver. "Ugh!"

Tuck's mind accepted the idea, but could find no immediate use for it. "I'll save that, Brigit. It clicked. There's just one more question. Why didn't Falkoner phone a doctor when he began to feel the effects of the arsenic? They're painful—excruciatingly so. Dryness of the throat, intolerable thirst, violent cramps, retching—".

The door leading to the staircase opened. A stubby man in a tight, dark, pin-striped suit stood there blinking at the glare of sunlight pouring in the windows.

"I should like to speak to Mr. Tuck," he said in an

orator's voice. "A Mr. Gufferty said I might find him here."

"I'm Tuck," Tuck said.

The stubby man slid smoothly across the cement floor, and Tuck found his hand cradled in a smaller, softer one. "I am Mr. Goli," the well-lubricated voice said. "I have come to get the particulars of this most distressing affair. Mr. Falkoner was my client and my friend."

FROODY and Brigit left, Brigit dragging back and watching over her shoulder like a child at bedtime. Froody with a dogged disinterest for anything but their search through the poison books.

"Have a cigar," offered Mr. Goli, smelling one and extending another.

"No, thanks. I'm glad you came. I had planned to get in touch with you. I have several questions which bother me. You may be able to answer them." Tuck opened his black notebook and then regarded Mr. Goli. "How did you learn he was dead?"

"The paper, Mr. Tuck. The paper. An item on page two, relating the fact that he had died suddenly and unaccountably, and that the police were making every effort—" He made an easy gesture. "The usual thing."

"Why," Tuck asked, "did he have two bodyguards?"

Mr. Goli regarded him with affability. "I've often asked myself that very question. I finally decided that it was a harmless eccentricity. He picked them both up on the beach, I understand."

"So do I," said Tuck. "But I don't understand why."

Mr. Goli leaned conspiratorially forward. "He was *extremely eccentric*," he confided, as one imparts a profound secret.

Tuck recoiled slightly from the subtle wave of perfume which wafted up from Mr. Goli's scrupulously oiled hair. "Was Mr. Falkoner afraid of someone?" he asked.

Mr. Goli looked genuinely amazed. "Afraid?" he asked, tilting his head to one side. "Afraid?" he repeated, tilting it to the other. "Of whom?"

"That," said Tuck, "is more or less what I asked you."

Mr. Goli considered his cigar narrowly. "You know," he said at last, looking up with an air of decision and frankness, "I've often asked myself the same question. Now there's just one possibility that occurs to me—and I'm afraid it's not worth much. There was a little incident about a year ago. Mr. Falkoner, purely as a side line, has for years dabbled in interior decoration. He has also decorated large homes when especially elaborate parties were to be given. A young actor—I needn't mention names, I'm sure, although should you ever have the slightest need for it, I would of course oblige—this actor was going to give a party, as a celebration after the premiére of his new picture. The elite of Hollywood were invited. The young actor, who knew Falkoner slightly, gave him *carte blanche*. His home, I understand, was rather impossible. He was the sportsman type and ran to elks' heads and leopard rugs, so Mr. Falkoner, very tastefully, decided to create of the place a bower of flowers, a bower, Mr. Tuck. I understand that everything impossible in the home was masked by young birch trees, painted maroon, and covered with gardenias. And there were loops of orchids about. Unfortunately, Mr. Falkoner, as a result I am sure of a misunderstanding, spent on the flowers alone what the actor had planned on spending for the entire party. When he got Mr. Falkoner's bill, he apparently went into a tearing rage, accused Mr. Falkoner of chicanery, and loudly threatened to—well, bluntly, to beat him to a pulp, and then to sue him in every court in the land."

Young birch trees, thought Tuck. *Painted maroon.* "Go on," he said.

"Mr. Falkoner came to me, of course. I assured him that the actor hadn't a legal leg to stand on, so of course all he had to worry about then was the prob-

lem of whether or not the actor would carry out his
threat of beating him to a pulp. It was just about that
time that the dark young man came to live with Falkoner. I understand that for a while he went everywhere with him. I guess Falkoner took a liking to the
boy, because the actor died a few months later of pneu-
monia, I believe. But Jim—I think that's his name—
stayed on. And then, a month or so after the actor
died, Tom—I *believe* that's his name—came." Mr. Goli
smirked. "Just one big happy family it's been, ever
since."

"How about André Viaud?"

Goli cocked his head. "Viaud? Viaud? I don't believe I know him. . . . Oh, yes, the Frenchman. Charming chap. I met him once. Why, he had a nervous
breakdown, I believe. Falkoner, you know, was rather a
vegetarian. I believe he thought he might help Mr.
Viaud. A charming gesture, I thought at the time. I
remember Mr. Falkoner saying to me, 'He's a genius,
Goli. People who are interested in mathematics all over
the world know about him. I met him sitting in a corner at a party. People pointed him out to me. And
look at him!' And he laughed."

"Who is Falkoner's doctor?"

"Oh, I don't think he had a doctor. Wait a minute.
I remember about two years ago he became concerned
with his weight. I have that trouble too, as I am afraid
you can see, and I recommended my doctor to him.
General practitioner, but wonderful on weight."

Tuck poised a pencil over his black notebook. "What's
his name?"

"Grispin." Goli stood on tiptoe to look across Tuck's
arm while he wrote. "G-r-i-s-p-i-n, Raymond. He's in
the Wilshire Medical Building."

"Do you know Mrs. De Lisle?"

"Regrettably, no. A charming lady, according to Mr.

Falkoner. He mentioned her several times, always with great fondness."

"Do you know Mrs. Morrissey?"

"Again, no. Although from what Earl said of her, she must be a delightful person. 'A real lady,' I remember he said of her once."

"Do you know of any reason why Mr. Falkoner chose such an out-of-the-the-way house to live in?"

"Tastes differ," said Mr. Goli with his easy gesture. "Myself, I prefer the feeling of people around me."

"When did you last see Mr. Falkoner?"

"This Thursday night at about nine-thirty."

"Oh?" asked Tuck.

"An unexpected visit, but of course a welcome one. He was a most stimulating personality, I always found."

"What did he come to see you about?"

"Well, it seems, although you may not believe it, I know I didn't, that two young writers, to whom he had extended the opportunity of working side by side with him, were planning to sue him. To *sue* him, Mr. Tuck. He was naturally concerned and came to me to see if the contract I had drawn would protect him. I assured him that it would. In any court in the land."

"Oh, I don't know," said Tuck. "Some judges are inclined to frown on speculative contracts."

Mr. Goli drew himself up to an oily five feet eight. He contrived to look both dignified and aggrieved. "That contract," he said, "protected my client against just such ingratitude."

"It sure did," Tuck agreed. "Did Mr. Falkoner eat or drink anything at your house?"

"Nothing, except a glass of water. Two, to be exact."

"Oh? And what would you say was his attitude? Was he unusually depressed? Upset? Angry?"

"He was upset, naturally. Two snakes he had taken to his bosom had bitten him. But when I assured him that he was safe from their fangs he relaxed and made several *bons mots*, I remember. Oh, but, before that, while he was drinking the first glass of water, he frowned. His frown—ah—I always rather noticed it. If you have ever seen him, you know that he had rather projecting brow ridges, and consequently, when he frowns, it's just a little bit—this is a personal opinion of course—it's just a little bit fearsome. He frowned, then, at the water, and said something to it."

"Said something to it?"

"Yes. It was either 'likker' or 'slicker.' I took it to be the latter, a reference to the two young men who had stooped to such a shabby means of extorting money from him."

"But, as a matter of cold fact they had a right, according to the contract, to expect $250 apiece upon completion of the play, didn't they?"

"At Mr. Falkoner's discretion," said Mr. Goli, "in the light of his judgment in the matter, providing the play was brought to a satisfactory completion—yes."

When Mr. Goli left, he pumped Tuck's hand again. After the door closed after him, Tuck drew a clean white handkerchief from his breast pocket and carefully wiped both palms. He left the scent of Mr. Goli hanging faintly on the air.

Then he telephoned to Dr. Raymond Grispin, and got him at the first try. "Did Mr. Earl Falkoner telephone you on Thursday night?"

The doctor sounded surprised. "That was a crazy thing. Yes, he did. Complained of abdominal pains. I went to him at once, left a poker game. Lord, but he lives a long way from anywhere. Got there, rang the bell, knocked, hollered, did everything but kick the door in. No answer. I went back to the poker game, knowing he could get in immediate touch with me again. No call. Remembering a couple of instances, I decided his pains had worn off, and he hadn't bothered to tell me so. Typical of the man. Nice fellow, I suppose. Healthy fellow. But as self-engrossed as all get out. It would never in God's green world have occurred to him to telephone and save me the trip."

"What time was it when he called?"

"Half past ten, exactly."

"And what time was it when you reached his house?"

"Quarter to twelve. Took me forever to find the place."

"Thanks, Dr. Grispin."

"Fine. Glad to oblige. What's up?"

"He's dead. Arsenic."

"Mother of Mary!" said Dr. Grispin. "Was that what was wrong! Mother of Moses! The coma had hit by the time I got there!"

"That's what I figure."

Tuck crossed the last question off his list, reflecting that Falkoner's isolated house had massed itself passively against him, collaborating in his death.

As he drove west toward Santa Monica, he thought that he was aping Froody's tactics. He was starting at both ends and working toward the middle. But until Froody and Brigit reached the middle, or rather, the name of the poisoner, there was nothing else that he could do except grope for answers to those annoying, intriguing questions about the dead man and his associates.

Let's see. Mrs. Lovelace said they always swim in front of the lifeguard station. Wilshire would be best. He thought of all the streets he had followed to find a solution at the end. At present, Wilshire Boulevard was better than those roads in his mind, leading nowhere.

The wide beach, with the wide sea sparkling coldly beyond it, was deserted. The small square Spanish building which in summer, he knew, would be surrounded by multicolored bathers, looked against the empty blue winter sky not quite real, like something the hands of a stage crew had erected. He descended the steps beside the lifeguard station, stepped into the cool sand, and immediately felt it sift into his shoe.

Tom was doing energetic push-ups, his lock of tan hair bouncing against his forehead: Jim was sitting propped against the pale gold stucco wall of the deserted building, reading a paper. Both men were startlingly tan, startlingly huge, and Tuck had the feeling that for the first time he was seeing them against a proper background. As a child, engaged in the busy importance of building a sand castle, looks more alive, more real than the same child at a desk in a classroom, so Jim and Tom were now manifestly themselves.

On seeing him, Tom stopped in the middle of a push-up, and then bounded lightly to his feet, brushing sand from his big hands. Jim looked up from the paper, folded it neatly, laid it beside him on the sand. As he stood up with the fluid and easy movement of an animal the afternoon wind took the paper and pushed it flat against the stucco wall against which Jim had been leaning, and then, playfully, tumbled it off down the beach.

Tuck had often found his unusual height of advantage to him. He used that advantage now, standing very straight so that he perceptibly looked down at the two big men before him. At the same time he was conscious that to an observer, had there been one, the triad would be amusing, and that he would be the most amusing element: a giant in a dark flapping overcoat, with a dark felt hat shading his eyes, standing rather pompously on the sunny, empty beach, his out-of-placeness contrasted by the two brown and almost naked men.

They stood watching him for half a minute, waiting for him to begin.

Then Jim said, "You want to talk to us?"

"Yes. I'm perfectly willing to do it here. On the other hand, I'm equally willing to do it at headquarters. You have the choice."

Tom started to speak, and Jim, without looking directly at him, turned his head slightly. "Shut up." And to Tuck: "We've told you everything we know."

Tuck shook his head. "No, you haven't. You haven't told me why Mr. Falkoner needed two bodyguards."

"He didn't," said Jim. "That was all in his head."

"We'll get in trouble—" began Tom.

Again Jim turned his head. This time he only looked at Tom. Tom collapsed into angry sullenness.

"Tom," said Tuck, "take a walk down to the pier. Don't take it into your head to bolt, whatever you do.

I'll be watching you while I listen to Jim. Then I'll listen to you."

Tom gave Jim a last long rebellious look, and then obediently turned and dogtrotted toward the dark skeleton of the pier, making a complete pivot in his traces every so often to look back at them.

"Now," said Tuck.

"Shall I begin at the beginning?" asked Jim.

" 'Begin at the beginning,' " quoted Tuck gravely, " 'and go on until you come to the end.' "

"I guess the beginning was when Mr. Falkoner invited me to have a carrot. That was back when he was working for the studio. He used to take a long lunch hour and come down and have a swim and eat his lunch out of a hamper while he was drying off. I was at the beach every day and got to know him by sight. Then sometimes he'd say 'Hello' and I'd say 'Hello,' and then after a couple of months, he asked me to have a carrot."

"When was this?"

Jim frowned as he tried to remember. "March, I guess. Last year."

"Go on."

"So while I was eating the carrot, he asked me was I a vegetarian—did I eat nothing but vegetables. I said I'd eaten a lot of things in my time, and not eaten a lot too, but when I could get it, meat was all right by me. He laughed a lot, like it was very funny. Then he gave me a piece of whole wheat bread with salad piled up on it and asked me what I did to make a living.

"I said nothing just then. I'd just got out from Texas with a little dough I'd earned this way and that, and was kind of waiting for something to turn up. He said, 'I come from Texas.' And I said he didn't sound like it, and he said, 'That was a long time ago.'

"Then he packed up his hamper and went away. But the next day he stopped me as he was coming up from the water and I was going to it and said, 'Jim, how would you like to work for me?' I said, 'What doing?' and he said, 'You'd be my secretary, sort of. Answer the phone, take my housekeeper to the market, run errands . . . ' I said, 'For how much?'

"He looked me up and down very quick, like he was trying to figure how much I'd expect, and then he said, 'Twenty-five a week and room and board.' That looked like really something, but I was working around for a lifeguard job which would be really O. K., so I said, 'For how long?' He got vague, and said, 'Oh, indefinitely, if I'm pleased with you,' but I knew that sort of answer, so I said, 'Well, I've got another job that's maybe coming up, only it would only be for the summer, so I got to know how long this will be for.' And he said, 'Oh, at least a year,' very impatient. So I said, 'O. K.' He said, 'I'll take you to my place tomorrow, so have your duds · packed, and where shall I pick you up?' I told him the Santa Monica Y.M.C.A. and he said, 'Be ready at one-thirty,' and went away. Then he looked back over his shoulder and said, 'Can you type at all?' and I said, yeah, pretty good, I'd taken it at night school, and he said, 'Swell.' "

Tuck looked down the beach and saw Tom nearing the pier.

"I can remember that part very clear. What he said, and all. The rest I don't remember so well. I went to work for him and the first thing I found out was that I was really his bodyguard. There was some actor laying for him about some deal. I told Mr. Falkoner that he could of told me on the beach about really being a bodyguard, that it wouldn't of scared me off the job, and he looked plenty sore at me guessing the real reason he didn't tell me. That was the thing about him, I found out. He never figured the other guy out quite smart enough.

"Well, I had stayed a couple months, and then I just happened to read in the paper about this actor dying. I knew Mr. Falkoner a little better by then, so I figured he might try to dust me off, and I was glad I'd gotten him to promise to keep me a year at least before I agreed to take the job.

"Sure enough, one morning he came in very cheerful to breakfast, rubbing his hands, and while he was tearing into the scrambled eggs—he did eat eggs—he said, 'Well, Jim, I guess I won't be needing you any more.' That made me sore. I'd just learned from a buddy that I was too late now to line up any lifeguard job that summer, but that I could of gotten one if I'd started in when he told me, just about the time I went to work for Mr. Falkoner. I said, 'But you told me the job was for a year.' He got very impatient and said, 'The guy's dead, Beaver. And I'm not worried about ghosts.' I got sore. Boy, I got sore. I said, 'You promised this job would last a year. I've done whatever you told me. You haven't any right to kick me out like this.'

"He said, 'Are you giving me orders?'

"I said, 'Yes.' Then we both said a couple more things. I got madder. I beat him up."

"Go on," said Tuck.

"So then he decided I didn't have to go after all."

"And then?"

"So then he hired Tom to protect him against me. He paid Tom the same as he paid me. I didn't mind. It was company."

"I suppose he met Tom at the beach too?"

"Yeah."

"Go on."

"Well, everything went along fine. My year was nearly up, but my typing was getting good. I felt pretty sure of getting a job easy. But then Tom chased Mrs. Lovelace with a knife for feeding his meat to the dogs. So I kind of fixed Tom."

"Wait a minute! You're not standing there and telling me that you beat him up?"

"Oh, no. I just got a scissors on him. She was a good cook. We'd lost two already, and she was the best of them all."

"Let me get this, please. Mr. Falkoner hired you to protect him against a man who then died, you beat him up, he hired Tom to protect him against you, and then you more or less beat Tom up. Is that it?"

"That's it," said Jim, his face utterly grave, his pale eyes untouched by any hint of laughter. "I didn't tell Mr. Falkoner about what I did to Tom. I like Tom O.K. and it was a soft job, twenty-five bucks a week, and nothing much to do but wash the dog once in a while."

Tuck threw back his head and laughed. When he sobered, Tom came trotting up, his face even ruddier than usual from exercise.

"Did he tell you?" he asked.

Tuck nodded.

"What's so funny?" asked Tom.

After dinner, André startled Laurel by leaning toward her ear from his place at the foot of the table and whispering, "Come up to my room with me." Then he straightened, gave a quick look at Tom and Jim, still eating, and said aloud, "I have a bottle of port."

"Port?" said Jeff. "Surely not port?"

"Port," said André loudly, and somewhat spoiled the effect by adding, "between the mattress and the springs."

"I'd *like* some port," said Woody.

André stood up, small at the end of the long table. "Jim, Tom?" he said, politely.

"Not me, thanks," said Tom.

"No, thanks," said Jim.

The four of them went up the narrow curved stairs. André's room quite suited him, Laurel decided. It was round, which made it unusual to start with. One narrow window looked out over the road, another over the garden. There were books everywhere, and a small radio with a separate turntable. The little bed looked almost like a child's bed. The folded afghan across its foot was the only really homelike touch she had seen in the house.

"Falkoner told me his mother knitted that," said André. There was something very like mirth in his eyes. "He offered to take it away, but I told him I liked it."

He folded back the mattress, Jeff and Woody assisting, and drew out the bottle of port. "A friend gave it to me for Christmas," he said. "I've been saving it for a special occasion. But we can use it to make a special occasion."

"A wake," said Woody.

"Glasses," said Jeff. "We forgot glasses."

He came up with four small tumblers. "No wineglasses," he reported. "A shame, because I have always believed that they make the wine taste better."

They sipped and talked and talked, and André and Woody exchanged a joke in French which they declared was not for feminine ears.

"Let's go for a walk," André said suddenly. He jumped up and went to the window overlooking the garden. "It's a wonderful night. California nights are unlike any others. There's a strange quality to them. Cold. Remote from human joy and sorrow. They make me think geologically. They make me think of what a short time we have been around." He held out his small hand. "Come on, Laurel!"

Jeff and Woody declined. They declined, they said, in order to finish the wine. *They look very wise*, Laurel thought.

She and André followed the earth road in front of the house, and took a branch that led them to a dead end that stopped at a skeletal fence with the lights of the city beyond it. They looked at the lights without talking. "The promised utopia of the last century," said André at last. "But only from here. Down there is the same dirt and sin and ugliness."

"Not quite," said Laurel. "Los Angeles has an excellent sewage system."

That broke his mood, as she had known it would. He turned to her. "Gold in the moonlight," he said, "your hair." He looked levelly into her eyes. His own were sparkling. "I feel like singing."

"*Allons, enfants de la patrie*," began Laurel.

"*Le jour de gloire est arrive'*," he joined in.

They joined hands and marched back along the road.

A car had driven up in front of the house while they had been gone. A black car.

"Why, Mr. Tuck is here," said Laurel.

Everyone was in the living-room—even Mrs. Lovelace. Tuck walked toward them and dropped his hand on André's shoulder. "I'll have to take you along," he said.

Laurel stared at him. "But why? What's he done?"

"Well," said Tuck, "ten days ago he bought a lot of arsenic." With a glimmer of saturnine humor, he added, "The trade name is 'Taps for Rats.'"

The heavy black sedan hurled itself solemnly down the curving road which would finally thrust them all into the lights of the city, and André into the steel shame of a cell in the central jail. No one said anything, not even Brigit, sitting in the back seat with Froody, the only one to whom the ride through the night was prosaic. Tuck glanced once at André. He was sitting pressed against the other door of the car, his hands clasped tightly between his knees, his eyes on the windshield. His face had the grave, accustomed sadness of an urchin's. After they had traveled for several minutes, he asked hopelessly, "May I smoke a cigarette?"

Tuck extended his own pack sideways toward him. "Push down on that button, and you'll get a light. It pops up in a second."

He glanced again at André's face, as the faint glow of the lighter warmed it and brought it out of the darkness. He thought he saw a mild look of surprise.

"You could tell us whatever you have to tell now, you know," Tuck suggested.

André Viaud's lips tightened into a slit of despair. "You wouldn't believe me," he said, and Tuck could hear wildness under the deliberate calm of his voice.

They drove in silence through the night again. After a minute of this, André asked, "Am I under arrest?"

"No," said Tuck. "You are 'being held for questioning.' "

And then Tuck reached out his big hand and turned on the radio. He twisted the dial until he picked up a thread of music, patiently adjusted until the thread swelled into the exquisite calm of Mozart's *Eine Kleine Nachtmusik.*

He looked over at André Viaud. His eyes were bright in the dimness, his mouth was twisted in a smile. He turned his body in the seat and looked at Tuck. "You are a most unorthodox American policeman," he said. "One hears of rubber hoses."

Tuck did not reply, because he was engaged in swinging the big machine around a horseshoe turn. They seemed to hang out dizzily above the lights of the city for an instant, and then the car settled back onto the road like some refractory animal which has decided not to bolt after all. "Am I?" he asked then.

"I want to tell you my story," said André, all in one breath. He looked doubtful. "It will take a little time."

"We have lots of time," said Tuck, and drove until he came to a semicircular parking space between the road and the lights below and beyond. Since it was Saturday night, two other cars were already parked there. Tuck's headlights picked out two young couples heads together, who turned white, impatient faces toward the encroacher.

"Turn out those lights!" a boy's voice called.

Tuck did. He turned off the radio as well.

He knew that Brigit was leaning tensely forward in the back seat. He knew that Froody was sitting dumpy and somewhat expectant beside her. He half turned so that he was facing the little Frenchman beside him. "I can believe nine impossible things before breakfast," he told André Viaud.

Again André's eyes brightened momentarily. He clasped his hands tightly on his lap, and began to speak in a quick, light voice which seemed to be running a race with a mind which whispered that its efforts were wasted breath.

"I met Earl Falkoner," he said, "five months ago. At a dinner party at the home of a French director I had known in 1929, in Paris. I noticed Falkoner, because he refused most of the food, and asked for a glass of milk instead of the excellent wine. He was quite unconscious of any rudeness.

"It was not until he had learned from the director that I was a mathematician that he showed any interest in me. I believe now that my smallness physically, coupled with a brain capable of certain feats which his could not perform, interested him.

"The first I knew of this was when he presented himself at my side and said, brusquely, 'I hear you've had a nervous breakdown.'

"I detest that phrase. I replied as coolly as possible that I had, according to my doctor, lived a little too close to my work for too long, and was in need of a short vacation, and that since my contract with Cal Tech provided for one at this time, I was taking it. I escaped from him as soon as possible.

"The director called me by telephone the next morning, and said that Falkoner had in all seriousness advanced the idea that it might be very good for me to be his guest for a while. He said Falkoner had pictured an idyllic existence of vegetables, milk, sun, fresh air. I laughed.

"Rather to my surprise, my friend said, 'I think it might be rather good for you. The man's a fool, but that's not the point.' He went on to say that he himself had suffered a similar collapse several years ago, and by living with a group of Left-Bank Americans, and being forced to fit into a life totally different from his own, he had found himself recovered in an amazingly short time. He pointed out that living at a distance from the university, apart from my usual friends and occupations, would probably make me fit for work again in a very short time.

"He finally convinced me. The only thing that bothered me was Falkoner's motive in offering such large hospitality to a stranger. My friend believed that he was a faddist, and that I made an admirable subject on which to prove his theories. This, I confess, appealed to my sense of humor. I gave up my flat, and moved into Falkoner's house.

"My first amusement at the man and his ménage soon changed into something else. Everything, you see, was too big for me. The dogs, the bodyguards, the chairs . . . I was Gulliver in the land of giants. I began to wish very much to get away.

"There was something else that made me want to leave. I soon saw that my friend's analysis of Falkoner's motive in asking me there was wrong. The true reason was subtler, and rather terrible.

"He was a stupid man in many ways, Mr. Tuck. And I think the greatest egotist I have ever known. But neither his stupidity nor his egotism prevented him from realizing that he had met a person with—shall we say more gray matter than his own? It troubled him, this knowledge. He had to prove to himself his superiority over me.

"In my case, his tactics were these. Having invited me to his home, he dictated my diet, my bedtime, my mode of entertainment—all masked by the pretext of friendliness. This became most annoying. I am not a great enough person to accept patronage from a man for whom I have no respect.

"And yet—this was the curious part—I could never stand up against him. When he presumed to take away my after-dinner coffee and give me a glass of milk instead, my whole being rose in revolt—and I was impotent against his size, his vast self-assurance, his hard eyes.

"It was most humiliating. Dislike of him, and his house, became an obsession with me. And yet I could not leave. This part is so hard to explain. I am a Frenchman. And I was in his house, eating his bread.

"It was at the dinner table, I remember, I suggested that I had accepted his hospitality for too long a time, and felt that I must go. He confronted me with his eyes and said, with friendly impatience, that I was talking nonsense, and that it was a big house and one more at table made no difference, that he was delighted to have me there, that there must be no more talk of going until I was well again.

"My desire was to say, 'I dislike you and your house and your dogs. I am not growing better for being here, but worse. And I am leaving tomorrow.' But I couldn't say it. I was like a child before a stern wise father—I could no more say those words than I could have committed myself to a physical struggle with him and come away triumphant. His blunt mind was pitted against my brain, which is a very different one, and his brain was victorious."

André Viaud looked up at Tuck. It was a dubious look. "Can you understand that?"

"Very well," said Tuck.

This seemed to give André courage. When he spoke to Tuck again his voice seemed brisker, and more assured: "That moment was a turning point. He sensed my impotence and took continual advantage of it. Life became unbearable. And he seemed to grow fat on his treatment of me. After he had humiliated me before his two henchmen at the table, he literally seemed to swell physically, as though he had been fed.

"And I retreated farther into myself, and was afraid of the thoughts I had. And then Miss Callender came in one night. She came in hoping to find Falkoner at home, and found only me. She asked me to be her escort for the evening. I agreed gladly. There were only two cars, and they were used by Falkoner and the two big men—it was very seldom that I was able to get away from the house.

"Miss Callender took me to several rather strange places. At one, I remember, there was a Negro in a white suit who stood in front of a small orchestra and beat three white drums with increasing savagery, until the sweat ran from his face. Then everyone applauded.

"I drank. I drank eagerly for the growing sense of freedom and self-assurance it gave me. But the evening remained incredible, like something out of a dream. I became drunk and still saw through to the essential futility of these sad gaieties.

"It was in a place called the Beachcomber's that my mind slipped away from me. Or rather, it became no longer my brain, but someone else's. Someone who was a stranger in my body. A cocky child, fearless and foolish.

"I had not thought of Falkoner for half an hour. Then Miss Callender mentioned his name, and an idea sprang into my head from nowhere. Or rather, into the child's brain that was taking the place of mine. I decided, calmly, astonished at the simplicity of the solution of my gnawing problem, that I would kill Falkoner.

"While Miss Callender went on talking—about him, I think—I sat there, seeing her red mouth moving, wondering how I would go about killing him. Recollection of his strength, his bulk, immediately brought to my mind the idea of poison.

"Miss Callender, seeing perhaps that I was not listening to her, abruptly suggested that we go home. I told her to go alone, that I had to think. I faintly remember saying that my mind had never been so clear. She laughed, and left me sitting there.

"Three Daiquiris had accumulated at my place. I drank them, one after the other, was chagrined at finding from the waiter that Miss Callender had paid the bill when she left, and went out of there into the night.

"The cold air did not sober me. It intoxicated me. I was careful to walk a straight, imaginary line I drew on the pavement with my eyes. I recall seeing a pair of women's feet go by with one red toenail showing at the opening at the tip of each shoe. I remember her voice saying, 'Drugstore.'

"I went into the first drugstore I came to, walked carefully under the lights. I went to the counter at the back and said, 'I want to buy some poison.'

"The pharmacist asked, 'Rats? Bugs? What?'

"I said, 'Rats.'

"And then he was presenting a box with a label showing a dead rat, its feet curled in the air. He spoke earnestly about it. I paid him, signed the book he pushed toward me, and went out, still walking the imaginary line.

"By that time I had decided to buy empty capsules, if possible, fill them with the poison, and wait for an opportunity to offer Falkoner one, as medicine of some sort. I decided to go to another drugstore for the capsules. I obtained them without any trouble.

"Then I called a taxi, and went back to Falkoner's house. I sat on the edge of my bed and filled all twelve capsules with the rat poison. I put them into an empty phenobarbital box. I went to bed, and slept for twelve hours. I woke up at noon, as sick as I have ever been.

"I have suffered *mal de mer*, and this was something like that, except that the physical nausea was accompanied by a mental nausea. A vast, troubling sense of self-failure. I did not remember the box of poison capsules until the day's end. And then the entire mad performance swept into my mind, and I was ashamed and also amused at the depths to which I had gone. I put the box of capsules into my coat pocket, intending to dispose of them in the lavatory.

"Intending also to get an album of music with which to calm myself, I went into the living-room. And there I saw three perfect strangers. Laurel Byrd, Jeff Prince and Woody Cornell. I had just learned who they were and why they were there, when I heard Mr. Falkoner's car drive up in front of the house, and so I went at once up to my room.

"The poison was still in my pocket, when Mrs. Lovelace called me to dinner. I went. I was not hungry, but I had no desire to have Falkoner come thundering up the stairs to my room to ask me why I was not dining.

"And then it happened. Falkoner suddenly pointed his fork at me, and commanded me to eat my dinner. And just as he did so, my hand stole into my pocket, and touched that box, and into my mind leaped the thought that at my fingertips was enough poison to kill him a dozen times. A wave of self-assurance swept through me. From that little box, up my arm, into my brain. I stood up. I said, 'No!' I went upstairs.

"I went upstairs on very light feet, I assure you. I was filled with elation. That, you see, was the first time in all the long months I had been there that I had stood my ground against him.

"A yearning for my own life took me. I made plans, up there in my room, to find an apartment near the university at once. And then, I remember, I thought: Now would be a good time to throw this poison away, while they're all at the table. But I found that I didn't want to throw it away."

André stopped talking abruptly, and ran a small hand through his shock of black hair. He looked sideways at Tuck, who was watching him gravely. He faced Tuck squarely and asked, "Do you remember Harold Lloyd in a picture called *Grandma's Boy?*"

Startled, Tuck confessed that he did not.

André went on: "I have always remembered that picture. As a young man, he was my favorite American cinema actor. I liked him even better than Chaplin. I saw all his pictures when I was living in Paris. French titles, with broad American slapstick. *Grandma's Boy* told the story of a coward. His grandmother, after seeing some of the plights his cowardice got him into, gave him a little carved ivory thing about three inches high, telling him that it was a talisman, the possessor of which became by its mystic power, capable of great bravery and daring. The coward, believing her, carried it with him, beat up the town bully, got the girl and, the picture being an American picture, a great deal of money, if I remember correctly. And then, at last, the little grandmother told him that he had been carrying in his pocket the handle of an old umbrella."

André gave a wry grin. "I tell you this so that you will not find yourself entertaining doubts as to my sanity, for I kept that box of arsenic capsules by me, Mr. Tuck, as a talisman. I knew that I would never poison Falkoner. Believe me when I say that. But that box of capsules had given me the power to defy him. It was the lucky penny, the four-leaf clover, the rabbit's foot. Most people, I think, have some talisman that sustains them through bad times. It may be a religious conviction, or a principle, or pride in their ancestors. But most of us have something.

"In fact, Mr. Tuck, I was afraid to throw away that box. The most sensible, the most unsuperstitious person in the world can harbor a lucky penny in his pocket. Because, while his intellect tells him the penny has no part in his good fortune, the thought edges into his mind that, should he throw away his talisman and then find his luck changed, he would *never be quite sure again*."

Tuck became conscious that Brigit was breathing into his ear, and that her arms were resting on the back of the driver's seat. He looked out at the lights below him, and the sharp small stars above. He looked at André, who did not seem to be breathing, but sat very stiffly in the corner of the seat, his eyes turned toward Tuck.

"But the capsule you gave Miss Byrd was really phenobarbital," Tuck said.

"Yes. I had put that box in my bathrobe pocket when I went down to the bathroom before retiring. I took one myself, you see, in order to sleep that night."

"And that was the box you gave to Dr. Day," Tuck stated.

"Yes."

"I know what you did with the box of poison," said Tuck. "Let me be sure I am right. You had just learned from Miss Byrd that Mr. Prince had gone to your room the day before, picked up from your bedside table the box containing the arsenic, and had offered it to a lady who could not sleep. A few minutes after you learned this, he shouted up to you to bring down the box, that there was arsenic in it. You thought, I imagine, that the police were waiting for you below. You were afraid."

"Yes," said André. "I threw the box of poison out the window. I brought the doctor the other box containing the phenobarbital."

Tuck nodded. Elation was tingling down all the nerves of his body. But his brain was cautious, and told him to ask one more question.

"You had some way of telling the two boxes apart. What was it?"

"I penciled a small cross in the lower right-hand corner of the box containing the capsules of arsenic."

Tuck reached out and turned on the ignition. The headlights of the car cut two bright tunnels of light through the night in front of them.

"But—" began Brigit, her voice full of excitement and confusion.

"F'gosh sakes!" called a boy's voice from one of the dark cars at the other side of the parking space. "Go home, why don't ya?"

Tuck put his long finger against the doorbell of the

dead man's house. He heard the melodious chimes sound within. He knew that in the next few minutes he would know whether André's story had been truth, or a magnificently elaborate lie.

Jim opened the door, and Tuck heard a flat voice—Mrs. Lovelace's voice—saying, "Foreigners—"

He heard an acid voice—Laurel Byrd's voice—say, "Mrs. Lovelace, do be still!"

He and André entered the brightly lighted living-room side by side, Froody and Brigit treading on their heels. All the faces in the room turned toward them. Tuck took a moment to look at each face, to see on which one André's return had wrought a change.

Laurel Byrd looked surprised, and then hopeful; she was regarding André steadily. Jeff Prince's eyebrows rose. Woody Cornell wore a look of bright interest. Mrs. Lovelace looked sulky. Tom grinned uncertainly. Jim's face remained expressionless.

Tuck walked toward Jeff Prince. He was aware that his feet made no sound on the thick rug, and that this added immeasurably to the suspense of the moment. He looked down at Jeff Prince who was leaning against the mantel of the fireplace, a cigarette raised to his lips. The blue smoke rose and curled on the air between his brown eyes and Jeff's blue ones. Then the young writer's thin hand make a quick arc and tossed the cigarette between the logs in the cold fireplace.

"Be very careful when you answer my question," Tuck told Jeff Prince. "Do you remember anything unusual about the box of capsules you got from Mr. Vjaud's room the day before Mr. Falkoner died?"

Prince's eyes followed a thought across the lamplit room to the wide view window, with the night pressing against it. He looked at the window for a full half-minute. No one in the room stirred. Tuck knew that Jeff Prince was seeing, against that black and shining pane, the mental image, greatly enlarged, of a square tan pharmacist's box, with a typewritten white label pasted in the center of the top lid.

Then he nodded once. "Yes," he said, "there was a small penciled cross in one corner. The lower right-hand corner."

And then, shrill and mundane, the telephone rang. As Jim rose to answer it, Tuck felt someone pluck his sleeve, and looked down at André's triangular face. "All right?" asked André.

"All right," said Tuck.

"Come with me to the window," whispered André. "There is something I can tell you now."

Jim re-entered the room. "For you, Cornell."

Woody, looking agreeably expectant, went out to the telephone.

André stood with his back to the room. He spoke so softly that no one else could possibly hear what he was saying. Tuck soon understood why.

"I have tried to keep in the background," André said. "I have said as little as possible, because I didn't want to be noticed. You know why that was. But this may be important. This may help you. At eleven on the evening Falkoner died, after everyone had gone, I was in the garden. You know why I was in the garden. You know that I went there too late. I heard the doorbell ring. But by the time I reached the door, the person who had rung had crossed the drawbridge and was already starting her car. I caught just a glimpse of her profile before the car leaped away. I had seen her only once before, but her coiffure is distinctive. I am quite certain that it was a Mrs. De Lisle." He paused. Uncomfortably, he added, "The door was not locked."

"Oh?" said Tuck. He turned slowly away from the window and saw Woody Cornell hurry through the archway.

"Jeff," he said, "Let me use your car."

"Sure. Or I'll be glad to drive you wherever you want to go."

"No. I want to go alone." Woody hesitated, a look of puzzlement on his round face. Then he looked at Jeff. "Harold's left Ruth. No note. Nothing. He just turned up missing. I want to see if I can help her."

Tuck walked to Woody's side. He had the curious sense of treading a path marked for him by circumstance, a path whose end he could not see.

"Perhaps," he said, softly, "I can help too."

Woody looked up at him, startled. And then sudden understanding showed in his face. He said, "You're wrong, you know."

Tuck said, "Shall we go?"

What struck Tuck immediately about Ruth De Lisle was the vagueness that clothed her every motion with incompleteness. When he rang the bell of her house, he heard the clicking of her heels as she ran to open the door. On seeing him, she fell back. Her eyes, after the first glance, did not quite look at him, but rather at something just beyond his shoulder. Her voice was empty when she said, "Won't you both come in?"

As she led them into the living-room, he noticed that her shoulders had the tired hump of an old woman's. She sank into a low chair, facing the painting of a Paris street, and forgot to ask them to sit down. With her hands lying clasped in her lap, she looked at the Utrillo. She raised one long hand and felt the coil of hair which went so well with the aquiline nose, and the habitual gesture was strangely meaningless. He noticed that her long black dress was unrelieved by any jewelry.

Woody sat down on the green sofa, and Tuck followed suit. Ruth De Lisle continued to look at the picture above their heads. Suddenly Woody leaned forward. "Ruth," he said, "when I was seven, you visited my mother. You brought me a globe of the world. I spun it, and it stopped, and my eyes fell on the Celebes Sea. And I wanted to go there." The intensity of his look brought her gaze to his face. "What can I do for you?"

"Nothing," she said. And then she was listening. Her shoulders straightened, and she leaned forward from the hips. Then she stood up and ran to the door. They heard her open it. They felt a faint cool drift of air curl around their ankles. They heard the door close, with the finality inherent in the sound of all closing doors. When she came back from the entrance hall, her shoulders were stooped again. Her hands went to her temples; the tips of her fingers pressed against them for a moment. "No one was there," she said softly. There was fear in her voice.

Tuck waited to speak until she had reseated herself in the low chair facing him. "Do you have any idea where he has gone?" he asked.

She shook her head. "None."

"Has he ever done this before?" he asked.

She shook her head. "Never."

"Do you have any idea *why* he has gone?"

She shook her head. "No."

Tuck framed his next words carefully. "Mrs. De Lisle, I've just learned something that changes the whole picture of Mr. Falkoner's murder."

At the word *murder* her eyes left the painting on the wall and looked straight into his for the first time.

"I've learned that the murderer didn't kill the dogs, and didn't try to kill Mrs. Morrissey. The only person the murderer killed or even wanted to kill was Earl Falkoner."

"Oh?" she said.

"Why did you go to his house at seven o'clock on the night he died?"

Her face didn't change. She still wore the high-eye-browed look that was almost stupid. "That was for Denise," she said.

"The door was unlocked, Mrs. De Lisle."

"Was it?"

Woody Cornell sat up stiffly. His voice was as soft as Tuck's when he said, "What are you suggesting, Mr. Tuck?"

"I am asking why Mrs. De Lisle visited his house on

the night he died."

"It was for Denise," Ruth De Lisle repeated. Tuck was gratified to hear more life in her voice. The vagueness had left her eyes. "You see, I had to know whether he was really going to marry her."

"She had already told you that, hadn't she? She told you that same afternoon, when you and she drank the sherry."

Ruth De Lisle shook her head. "You don't understand. I had to find out if *he* was going to marry *her*."

"Why?"

"I don't think he loved her."

"But she is very rich."

"Yes. I wasn't sure, though, that he would have married for money, Mr. Tuck. He was sophisticated enough to know the wife has the upper hand in that sort of bargain."

"So you went to his house to find out?"

"Yes. Because I didn't want to tell her the truth about him unless I had to. She loves him, you see."

"I see. You're very fond of Mrs. Morrissey?"

"No."

"But you were willing to visit a man you disliked in order to spare her a possible hurt?"

"You don't understand. I've known her for such a long time."

Tuck saw the vagueness beginning to fill her mind again. She raised her hand to the coil of hair and felt it, carefully. Then she stiffened in her chair, and again leaned forward, listening.

"Mrs. De Lisle," said Tuck, "do you see why your husband might have left you?"

Ruth De Lisle sat very quietly in her chair, looking at Tuck. She stared at him for a long while, and when she had completely grasped his meaning, her face had subtly altered. The brows were less highly arched, the chin a little firmer and there was a pinched look to her nostrils.

"Why did you come here?" she asked him. "Is there something you want me to say? I've explained every-thing, as well and as truly as I could."

"I wanted to ask you this question, Mrs. De Lisle. Do you think Denise Morrissey killed Earl Falkoner?"

He felt Woody move abruptly on the sofa. He was sure his mind was full of the words, *Be careful, Ruth. Be careful!*

"No," said Ruth De Lisle, "I do not."

"Ah," said Tuck. "But if she learned bluntly and suddenly that he was not in love with her—?"

"I didn't tell her that."

"But if she learned that somehow?"

"No, she wouldn't. And I know. Because of the other time."

"Go on," said Tuck.

"Just after we graduated from high school. She met a man. At a church supper. In Pomona, in 1916, that was the only place you could meet a man."

"I remember Pomona, at about that time," Tuck said. "Blue laws, quiet streets, pepper trees, and all around, miles of orange groves."

"The main drag," she went on. "Horstwagg's Phar-macy, the hub of the town. Dancing school, and long Sunday dinners. A great many towns are like that still. I hope I never have to live in one."

"And so she met a man."

"Yes. A San Francisco young man. He had inherited an orange grove. He'd come down to look his property over. He lived with a relative who had one of the largest houses in town. I don't remember her young man very well. But I do remember his air of condescension. That was partly Pomona's fault. It was the sort of small town that people who weren't born there passed through to get somewhere else."

"So she fell in love with him."

"Yes. I saw then what it was going to be. She was local talent, the best he could hope for. I always knew that he would go home and forget her fast. She didn't. I saw them once, coming hand in hand out of his orange grove. There was a fine moon, and the trees were in blossom. You could smell them for miles. You became impregnated with that heavy odor. I remember Denise's face in the moonlight, white and almost beautiful. I remember how he looked down at her and smiled."

"What happened?"

"Somehow, perhaps because she wanted so much to believe it, perhaps from something he said to gild a moment among the orange trees, she became convinced that he wanted to marry her and take her with him to San Francisco. I was the only one, fortunately, that she told this to. I didn't have the cold courage it would take to disenchant her. She told me this on the porch of her father's house—a little clapboard house it was, painted gray, with a deep cold cement porch and deep eaves. Most of the houses were like that. Oh, and with pots of asparagus fern on the cement steps leading to the porch. And a hydrangea bush each side of the steps. You know, long dark green leaves, and those great balls of weepy blue blossoms. During all the years I didn't see Denise, while Harold and I were living all over Europe, I never thought of her without thinking of those hydrangea bushes. Where was I? Oh. It was on that porch that she told me she had packed a bag, and was meeting him in the drugstore right after dinner. That would have been about six-thirty. Everyone ate as early as possible, and then went to bed early, because the evening was so long.

"I passed the drugstore at eight, on my way home from the library. I glanced in, and between the great globe of green water and the globe of red, I saw her sitting there at the long counter. That waxy purplish-brown marble. She was sitting there, with her eyes on the clock. There was an ice-cream soda in front of her, and an empty glass beside it, with the straw bent limply over the edge. As I looked in, she lowered her eyes from the clock, picked up the long spoon, and began to eat the ball of pink ice cream, slowly and carefully.

"I went past. But after I got into bed, I remembered that her father had gone to a dentist's convention. I began to think of her alone in that little house, unpacking her suitcase. I got dressed and went there. I rang the bell for a long time. The phonograph next door was playing, 'It's a long way to Tipperary.' Then the door opened suddenly, and she was standing on the other side of the screen door, in a long white nightgown. She made me think of Ophelia.

"She said, 'He didn't come.' Before I could speak, she added, 'I drank four strawberry sodas.' I tried to say something, but she spoke first. She said, 'I just drank a glass of insecticide.'

"I remember running for the doctor, and the smell of the orange blossoms, and that invincible victrola going on and on. And I remember her eyes looking up at the doctor from her bed, and they were pale and weepy like those hydrangea blossoms."

"I see," said Tuck.

"So that's why I went to Falkoner's. I was sure he had no intention of marrying her. If he hadn't, there was no need for me to tell her what I knew about him—that he was a cheat, and a small one at that. But if I learned that he did intend to marry her, I was going to tell her the truth about him. I felt that I owed her that, because we had been young together in 1916."

"So when you came back from Falkoner's, and learned from Mr. Cornell about the arsenic, you thought she'd gone and done it again."

"Yes. When I met her again in Naples with her husband, I didn't see much of the girl I had known. But I believe that people remain the same, in spite of the changes time seems to make. I thought that somehow— I didn't know how—she had found that Falkoner didn't care for her. I thought that she'd been left waiting at the long brown marble counter again, and again had tried to end her grief. You see, Mr. Tuck, she didn't love her husband. She told me that quite blandly. But very few women can escape love because they are afraid of it. The first time I saw her with Falkoner, I knew that Denise was in love for the second time in her life."

"It's a little too simple, too black-and-white, somehow," said Tuck.

"It would be, with Denise. She's an extraordinarily simple person. Simple, and shallow, with hydrangea bushes each side of the steps, and deep eaves." She added, "I'm not being flippant."

Tuck saw that talking of a loss other than her own had done her good. When she stood in the doorway saying good night, she looked down at the rectangular pools of water and said firmly, "When Harold comes to his senses, we're going to sell this house. It's too big for two people." Then she turned to Woody. "Stay here with me for a little while. I'm all right now, except I'll still keep hearing him at the door."

Tuck telephoned the house on the hill. He asked for André. "Look, Viaud, when you threw the arsenic capsules out the window of your room, how many were in the box?"

"Ten."

"Did you count 'em?"

"No. I have a camera memory."

"Explain that, please."

"I am one of those people who can look at a table containing forty small objects and can tell a week later how many teeth were missing from the comb, and exactly what time the watch said. I poured the capsules out of the box into my hand. I glanced at them for perhaps half a second before I threw them out the window into the garden. There were ten."

"And you had bought a dozen empty capsules?"

"Yes."

"And filled them with *Taps for Rats?*"

"Yes."

"Thanks," Tuck said, and hung up the receiver. He edged out of the phone booth wondering if any jury in the world could be made to believe in the validity of the camera memory.

Denise Morrissey was wearing a simple black dress with a fluffy white collar. She had been playing solitaire. The cards were laid out on the coffee table, black on red. As she sat down, she swept them up with her small pink-nailed hands and tapped them twice against the glass of the table. She slid the pack into a little leather case, and snapped it. "Is there anything I can do for you?" she asked. Her voice was pleasant and just a trifle condescending.

"You gave Mr. Falkoner $1,000," Tuck said.

She put the card down on the edge of the table. "Yes, I did. Is that all you wanted to know?"

"Why in cash?"

"He asked for it that way."

"A thousand dollars is a lot of money," Tuck said.

She looked somewhat amused. "I thought so once myself."

"What story did he tell you when he asked for the money?"

"No story at all! It was a friendly business arrangement. He needed that much money to pay the writers who were working on the play. By supplying that money I had a quarter interest in the play. He never sold a story for less than $10,000."

"That could mean also that he'd never sold a story," said Tuck.

"I really can't imagine why you're here," Mrs. Morrissey replied candidly.

"I'm here to arrest you for the murder of Earl Falkoner."

She stared at him in astonishment. "Over $1,000? Oh, come now, Mr. Tuck. You seem too intelligent really to believe a thing like that."

"No," agreed Tuck. "Not over $1,000. But when you walked into his house, and learned that the writers had never seen any of that $1,000, that he'd cheated the two other writers, you got for the first time a very ugly picture of Mr. Falkoner. If he had cheated you, you knew that he didn't love you. You knew that if he married you it would be for money, not for love, and that's what you killed him for."

She leaned toward him. She spoke distinctly, carefully.

There was no mistaking the fact that she was telling the truth. "Mr. Tuck, I didn't kill him."

Tuck made a guess, based on what the dead man had said to his glass of water when he went to Goli's house after leaving Denise and before going home to die. Tuck guessed that he had said, "Liquor!"

"But he drank a glass of champagne here the night he died," he said, with great assurance.

"Certainly," she agreed smoothly. "It was all I had to offer him. I had just returned from the East. It was that or chicken soup."

"He never drank. Why should he drink champagne with you?"

"He did it to please me," she said. "There was no poison in the champagne, I assure you."

"But there was. I've just learned, you see, that those two capsules you took from the box at his house had arsenic in them, after all."

The painted lips parted as the muscles of her jaws went slack with shock. Slow horror gathered in her eyes; the skin below them tightened into two fans of fine lines.

They sat there staring at each other.

Then Denise Morrissey stood up, looking sideways at nothing from narrowed eyes.

Tuck stood up too and watched her turn and go with accelerating steps across her luxurious rented room to a door at its far end.

And suddenly, he found himself thinking of the last act of *Hedda Gabler*. The shot from the other room. He followed swiftly after her. He stood watching her cross a peach and green bedroom. She opened a closet door. He tensed.

She drew a mink coat from a rack and hung it on her shoulders. Holding it close about her throat with one hand, she slipped the other into the pocket. He peered for the bulge of a little ladylike revolver.

"I am going to my lawyer," she said, in a clear, lady-like voice.

Tuck relaxed. "Allow me to drive you." She nodded once.

He preceded her to the front door of her apartment, opened it, and stood aside for her to pass him. She went through the door holding the coat tight about her throat with one small hand, her shoulders straight, and in her eyes, a plan.

"Until Ruth De Lisle told me that Denise Morrissey took poison for her lost love in Pomona in 1916, I wasn't quite sure," he told the three young faces before him. "Then I knew. The difference between what she did then, and what she did when she lost Falkoner, lies in the difference between a girl of eighteen, and a woman of forty. The girl's anguish was directed against herself. The woman's against the man. The reason? Ten years of marriage to a rich, ugly little producer named Joel Morrissey. Denise Hooper and Denise Morrissey were a couple of different fellows, you see."

Laurel sat down abruptly on the suitcase at her feet. "But I don't see," she said.

"Neither do I," said Jeff.

"Nor I," said Woody Cornell.

Tuck sat down in a red chair, and leaned back. Enthroned, he looked at them, and then closed his eyes. "I was sure for a while that Denise Morrissey hadn't killed Falkoner, because of the dead dogs. She had no opportunity to poison the dogs' meat when she visited the house on the afternoon of the day before he died. And she couldn't have poisoned them later because she was being hauled out of the grave by Dr. Day, and a nurse was with her the next day until six o'clock. That evening, Falkoner visited her at seven. And she couldn't have poisoned them after he left, because, disregarding her weakness after a siege with acute arsenic poisoning, the medical examiner found meat with the poison in the dogs' intestines, which means that according to what knowledge I had, they were poisoned at about six, when

Jim fed them.

"And so they were. Because it was a very little while before six that André Viaud, trapped in his tower room, threw ten capsules, each containing a fatal dose of arsenic, out the window into the garden where the dogs—and you have told me that they were perpetually hungry—saw them lying scattered on the grass, and ate them. And died."

"It seems odd to me that a mathematician would do anything quite so childish," said Jeff.

"Are mathematicians shockproof?" asked Tuck. "Think of it from his point of view. No sooner did he learn from you, Miss Byrd, that a woman had taken home arsenic which he had bought than you, Mr. Prince, hallooed to him to bring down that box of arsenic at once. He felt a rope around his neck. He knew that his strange story about the purchase of the poison would be believed by no one. He knew that even his closest friends would think of his recent breakdown, and decide along with the police that he had intended to kill Falkoner, and that his plan had gone astray. Then he saw the open window, and the big empty garden below, and did desperately the only thing he could to save himself. You see, he hadn't heard Dr. Day's story. He thought that Mrs. Morrissey was dead. And so the box he brought down to Dr. Day contained only phenobarbital.

"And Mrs. Morrissey? Remember you told me, Miss Byrd, that Rita Callender kept saying, 'How terrible you look, darling!' Of course she looked terrible. She had made up her mind to marry Falkoner. She had just told her oldest friend so. She had just walked into his house, and had learned almost at once that he had cheated her out of $1,000. If it had only been more, he might be alive now. But $1,000! In what harsher, more positive way, do you think, could a wealthy woman learn that she was not loved?"

"But how did she know what Harvers was talking about?" asked Woody. "She learned that Falkoner was a cheat, I'll grant you that. But how could she have known that Falkoner had cheated *her?*"

"I think you told me, Miss Byrd, that Harvers mentioned the title of the play you three had been working on. In your detailed description of that afternoon, I think you told me that Harvers said, '*That Was Yesterday.* Lousy ·title.'"

"Yes. I did."

"That's how she knew," said Tuck. "And does anything else about that title occur to you? No? It's just exactly the title that a shrewd man would pick to catch the interest of a woman of forty."

"But I want to know what happened," said Laurel. "How did she do it?"

"Oh," said Tuck. "That. That you'll have to take my word for. No one was there, except Mrs. Morrissey and Mr. Falkoner. He's dead, and she is not talking— she has a very good lawyer. But this is what happened.

"All the long day after the ordeal with the arsenic— and the vomiting, and the washings out of her stomach— she lay in her apartment and thought about Falkoner. The fact that the nurse—who may have been a bit of a Sairey Gamp—suggested champagne didn't help any. Because Mrs. Morrissey never drank. And for her champagne was heady stuff. And the tipsier she got, the less was she able to control her emotions. And the nurse left, and the gardenias came. Those gardenias are important. Because, you see, they had been bought with her money. A rather acid drop in her cup, I think those gardenias were.

"And then Falkoner came. And she accused him. She accused him—and perhaps cried a little—of cheating her. She accused him, hoping against hope that he would have a plausible answer.

"And Falkoner underestimated her. He saw the weepy blue eyes, the little hands, the blond hair, and underestimated her. He told her a tale she could not swallow.

"I think that for the sake of her pride she pretended to believe him. She may have asked him to bring her purse to her—I think she was lying down on the sofa, with a gold quilt over her. Or she got her purse herself. That doesn't matter. But I've noticed that when the scene is over, the decision made, the die cast, women always put on fresh lipstick. I think that she opened her purse, and saw the other capsule." He looked hopefully around at them. "I am right in believing that none of you saw her take two capsules?"

"I was watching her face," said Jeff.

Laurel and Woody shook their heads.

"Viaud's word will have to do, then. There were only ten in the box you gave back to him, Miss Byrd."

"But couldn't someone else have taken the other capsule? The box was in plain sight on the mantel all the next day," Woody pointed out.

"But you see, by the time Dr. Day came and said there might be poison in the capsule, André had already taken the box upstairs."

"Go on with Mrs. Morrissey," commanded Laurel.

"She opened her purse then, and saw the other capsule. And then into her little tipsy mind there leaped a plan. A test. A final test. She excused herself, left Falkoner sitting in one of her brocade chairs, congratulating himself at having pulled through a bad mess. She went into the kitchen and opened a bottle of champagne. She filled two glasses. And into one she unscrewed the fine white crystals in the second capsule. That was the glass she offered Falkoner, hoping that he would refuse. Because if he had refused, if he had said, 'But you know I never drink,' she would have believed his story about her $1,000. If he took the champagne, she knew it would be for only one reason. To please her. To give in on a small point, in order to placate. And that's what he did. And I think she watched him drink without a twinge of remorse or fear. And I think she thought of a young man who left her waiting in a drugstore in 1916."

"The simple soul, with a fixed idea," said Woody suddenly.

"Exactly," said Tuck.

"But when you questioned her!" Laurel said. "Didn't something show?"

"No," said Tuck. "Because when I questioned her, she quite honestly believed that she hadn't poisoned him at all!"

"You mean she *forgot?*" Jeff exclaimed.

"No. No, it was like this. She woke up with a hangover, and the conviction that she was a murderess. Very few people, I think, have spent a morning like that morning of Mrs. Morrissey's. And then, confirming her worst fears, Rita Callender phoned her and told her Falkoner was dead. Remorse? Yes, I think so. Fear? More of that. And then—and then, preserving Denise's life pattern, a pattern she made for herself by marrying a rich man, Dr. Day came and told her that there had been no poison in the capsule she took! Think of the relief! The escape into her pattern again. Chastened, perhaps. And able to believe with honesty that Rita Callender had killed him out of drunkenness because she herself had so nearly done so. And then she bought a black dress, and perhaps felt really sorry for him, and played solitaire."

There was silence in the room. The afternoon sunlight was bright on the furniture. Laurel noticed irrelevantly that the round needle box by the turntable was open, and empty once more.

"I'm thinking of a woman sitting at the far end of a bar in Shanghai, with a jeweled butterfly in her hair," Woody said quietly.

"Well," said Jeff, and his smile was wry, "I met a Borgia after all. And fell for her, hard."

"I'm sorry for her," Laurel said. "She loved him."

"But she killed him," Tuck reminded her.

"How do you know it happened that way?" Jeff asked suddenly. "She had two capsules, I'll grant that—"

"Women do that with medicine," Laurel said sagely. "They think that if one will do them good, two will do twice as much good." And suddenly she had the odd feeling that she had said that before. She tried to remember when and where.

"She had the opportunity," Jeff went on. "He was there, the champagne was there, the poison was there. But how can you be sure she did it?"

"He's dead," said Tuck. He added, "I only hope the attorney for the defense doesn't make too much over the buttermilk, as a possible means of administering the poison. That buttermilk has haunted me—"

"What buttermilk?" asked a voice.

Tuck jumped a little in his chair. Tom and Jim, in bathing shorts, came through the door that led up from the terrace. Tuck got out his little black notebook. "You two had better tell me what your new address will be."

"We're going to stick around for a while," said Jim. "Until they move the furniture, anyway."

"What buttermilk?" asked Tom again.

"The buttermilk Mr. Falkoner drank the night he died."

"Oh," said Tom. "But he didn't. I drank it."

"But you don't like buttermilk!" Tuck said.

Tom's head tilted slowly to one side. He thought. He looked back at Tuck. "No," he agreed. "No, I don't, come to think of it."